Jackson Wild

Soldier

Published by New Generation Publishing in 2022

Copyright © Jackson Wild 2022

First Edition

ISBN   978-1-80369-287-6

www.newgeneration-publishing.com

New Generation Publishing

In honour of the Veit brothers, Fritz, Otto and Walter, who, although German, have a story very much the same as ours.

Author's Note

In the First World War, many men died on the front line; and men, women and children back at home. I am writing this book for all of those innocent souls who lost their lives. However, if there are any references to a relative you might have had, please don't take it personally. I can assure you that I have not done this intentionally. And bless you if your relatives had to or will have to go through the experiences that the characters in this book lived through.

For all the lost soldiers in the Great War who we will try to remember.

Jackson Wild
February 2022

The News

I was doing a shopping errand for Mother when I saw it. Pasted onto a wall was a poster with the newly appointed Minister for War, Lord Kitchener, a bushy moustache across his top lip, looking down at me.

I noticed lots of men looking at the posters and flyers that had spread across the pavement. Lord Kitchener's patriotic face seemed to be staring at me in particular. I stared deep into his eyes. Could England really need that many men for the war I'd heard about? I would ask Father about it. He would know as he was in the army. I walked back down the street to my house.

My brother Harley was sitting in a tree, his eyes pressed to a pair of binoculars.

'Where are you?' he muttered to himself. I opened the wooden gate leading into our garden.

'Where's who?' I asked, climbing up next to him on the tree. He was gazing in the direction of the park.' He paused for a moment. 'Aha! There he is. Mr Bennet. He's talking to a group of young men. Must be trying to recruit some soldiers. You know, being a major and everything. Probably thinks he's going to get promoted because he'll suddenly show up with a bunch of men.' He kept his binoculars focused on Mr Bennet.

I figured it would be a good idea to bring up the idea of the oncoming war if he didn't know about it. Harley had always wanted to be a soldier. His dream was to wear a smart uniform with the Victoria Cross polished and pinned to his chest, pacing in front of a group of men, his chest puffed out, bearing the name Captain Tuck. Not too high, not too low, just high enough to be able to have your own say, he said. I decided better of it. He would find out in his own way.

'Is Fred home?' I asked. 'I need to ask him something.' Without answering Harley jabbed his thumb at the house. I climbed back down the ash tree and jumped off the lowest branch. When I entered the kitchen, Mother and Father were in; so was Fred. Like me Fred was short for his real name, Frederick. He said it was too posh a name, so he insisted he be called Fred, which was the same reason I insisted I was called Alfie, not Alfred.

'Have you heard the news?' Fred asked immediately, as soon as I came into the room. I nodded. 'I knew it,' Fred said. 'I knew Germany or some other stupid country would want to get involved in this fight between Serbia and Austria-Hungary. All these European countries are at each other's throats. And now we have to fight a country with a navy nearly as strong as ours. I bet France will be half controlled within the month. And that's just across the Channel from here.'

I stood there shocked. Whenever something that interested Fred was in the papers he borrowed from Father he was completely enwrapped. He would read the same article for days, devouring every word of it. The more newspapers that were interested in the subject the better. He used all his savings from his job at the local post office to buy week-long subscriptions at the newsagent.

But there was a question that had been nagging me.

'How old do you have to be to sign up?' I asked. I figured my age, seventeen, would be around the youngest that would be legal.

'I think it's seventeen or eighteen. And the oldest age where you're forced to go is around forty.'

I went to pour some dog food into the bowl of Mango, our black and white dalmatian. I then got a chicken thigh and chopped it all up. Mango liked chicken with his beef kibble. I then poured water on top of it all so that it was wet, which Mango also liked.

Harley had come inside, the leather string attached to the binoculars hung around his neck. 'Did you see Major Bennet? He was talking to all the lads down in the town. Wonder what he's up to?' He obviously didn't know about the war if he'd spent his day perched in a tree watching an army officer talking to possible recruits. He took his seat and began reading his book, Robinson Crusoe. Fred began to read a newspaper about the early stages of the war. I began assembling a miniature catapult. I was good at crafting with my hands. In five minutes I had finished it already and was loading it with small pieces of meat to fire at Mango. I took aim and fired. It nearly hit Harley who ducked. As he did so he glimpsed part of the headline on Fred's newspaper:

England Declare War on Germany

When Harley scanned the headline he looked as calm as ever. Mother and Father must've decided to let Harley find out the news by himself. He always found things out in the end.

'I knew you were hiding something,' he said quietly. He looked at Fred. 'I saw you exchange one of Mr Render's newspapers. I was using my binos so I could just make out one word: war.' Fred looked around guiltily. Father gave Fred a stern look.

'Is this true, Frederick?' Father asked.

'Yes, Father,' Fred replied. 'But I was very interested. And Mr Render is an old grumpster who's always grumbling about what time we deliver it. Says he wants it for his morning cup of tea, just after half seven.' Fred must've been one of the riskiest employees the post office had ever had. Mind you a lazy one too. Half the time on a Saturday he was late and was always getting ticked off for being untidy.

'Fred you shouldn't have done that,' Father told him. 'And Harley, you shouldn't have been spying on people.' Neither Fred, nor Harley looked very ashamed. It was just like both of them to do such a thing.

'Right,' Father cleared his throat. 'That's that. Let's not talk of this matter anymore.' Father sighed and hobbled towards the sitting room, meanwhile lighting his pipe. Mother started to make dinner. I continued to launch tiny pieces of meat in the air for Mango to catch. Fred and Harley resumed reading. We hadn't even properly talked about the thing that I could now not get out of my head: the war.

The next day I went to the Albert to have a drink. I always did when I was depressed and I wanted to laugh. I would laugh and laugh in those days. I didn't touch strong stuff like gin or rum until I was much older, but I liked beer. And occasionally a shot of whiskey.

It was as crowded as ever in there and I felt happy almost immediately. I ordered a pint of beer and sat down on a stool.

'Alright, geezer,' I heard someone say behind me. I looked and saw my mate Lenny's older brother Wilfred standing there.

'Alright, Wilf,' I said. 'What's you doin' here?'

'Oh y'know,' he replied, 'having a whiskey, playing a few cards. I'm a decent gambler. C'mon lad. Why don't you play with the men?'

'Alright,' I said. For some reason I could never resist playing cards, probably because I wasn't bad at it myself. I never should've done it though. It was a mistake that I regretted instantly.

Wilfred's friends welcomed me like a friend but didn't treat me as such. They cheated, the drink making them rude and boastful. Then the subject of war was brought up.

'Did you hear the news up in the town?' one of his friends said. 'We're at war with the blimmin' Germans. Can you believe it? Just cos Belgium got invaded. Dunno why they're so bothered?'

'Because,' another of his friends said, 'everyone loves little Belgium.' They all cackled with laughter.

'All right,' he said seriously now. 'Ten bob I sign up right now and give them the Fritz a run for their money.'

'Deal,' one agreed. Then to my surprise he got up and left the pub there and then.

'Lordy,' the one who'd taken the bet gasped. 'I didn't expect that.' He left the pub accompanied by all of his other mates. Wilfred rolled his eyes. 'Show off,' he muttered. He straightened up and laid an ace on top of the cards. 'I believe I win anyway.' And he left me to get another beer.

I downed the rest of my pint and ordered another one. I stayed there for a little while longer listening to all of the chatter. The barman seemed somehow fidgety whilst he served drinks.

I continued to drink my beer before I slammed my pint glass on the bar and left the pub.

Opening Stages

The whole town of Penge soon became engrossed in the war's opening stages. The British Expeditionary Force (B.E.F) had landed in France and were desperately trying to halt the German advance. But with little success.

I had seen the lists of casualties in the newspapers and whenever I went into town I would see a soldier or two strolling around or having a drink in the pub.

Much of Europe was mobilising its armies for a war. I didn't think the Germans would reach London – and Penge was on the outskirts of the capital, after all – if we put our backs into it. Nobody seemed to take the war that seriously though. They believed it would be over by Christmas and the Germans would be in disarray. Everyone thought that. I have to admit, I thought so too. That proved to be one of the biggest miscalculations of my life.

I once saw a company of soldiers marching through the town, buttons and buckles polished and gleaming, marching in perfect formation, saluting their officers.

I thought they looked simply grand. Harley did too. I thought he would go and sign up right then and there, even though he was still only fifteen. Of course he didn't though. He said it one evening in late August. Although it was the summer it was pouring with rain and no one wanted to go outside so we were all sitting around at home.

'I'm not going off to war unless I go with you,' he said suddenly.

'You're not going at all until you're of age, Harley,' Mother told him.

'Well, I am,' Harley retorted. 'But only if you lot go.'

'No, Harley,' Mother insisted, 'you're not going until you're of age and the war will be over by then.'

'I know that,' Harley told her, 'which is why I'm going sooner than that. I don't want to miss out on the fun.'

'It's not fun,' Mother said. 'It's bloodshed.'

'The smaller I am, the longer I'll survive,' Harley sang cheerfully.

Father chuckled and put some tobacco in his pipe.

'Brave little one you are,' he leant over and ruffled Harley's hair.

I ignored him and took out a little set of tools which I played about with whilst Mother and Harley bickered.

The newspapers never seemed to have good news.

I plucked the paper off the kitchen table and sat down to read it. I stifled a yawn and peered at the headline.

'What does it say?' Fred asked. 'Anything good?'

'Dunno,' I replied. 'It says "British Expeditionary Force clashes with Germans at Mons." Dunno what to make of that.'

'Probably bad,' Fred predicted. 'All of our stuff is.'

'If we don't make a stand soon,' Father told us, gulping down some tea, 'we're going to end up worse than we started.'

'See what I mean,' Harley said. 'They need me.'

'No, they don't,' I said, buttering a slice of bread.

'Why?' Harley asked.

'We've already got our lads out there,' Fred explained. 'It would only make us look bad. Imagine a load of lads our age attacking highly trained Fritz. It's almost laughable.'

I dipped my bread in my boiled egg and stuffed it in my mouth.

'Don't you worry, Harley,' Father reassured. 'We've just started a new way of putting battalions together. We're calling them pals battalions. It's a real winner. We've got sixteen hundred men, all of them pals and they're fighting together. Morale is high and we'll beat the Germans, don't you worry.'

Harley harrumphed and went back to his egg.

'Still,' he tried, 'I thought they wanted manpower. I'm only two years too young; that's not exactly a lot, is it?'

'Yeah,' I said, 'but imagine a person who doesn't even shave charging into battle.'

'I say,' Harley said, 'as long as you're fit and healthy and you're willing, that should be good enough.'

'But Kitchener says no!' Father told him.

'Can we please talk of something else,' Mother said. 'It's very tiresome.'

It was the only thing people were thinking about. I occasionally worked at a little workshop, fixing farm machinery and things like that. Whenever I went to the workshop my boss Mr Plide was constantly staring at the newspaper, while I fixed a few loose cogs or gears. At the pub, everyone was talking about it, even me!

I often went to the stream running through Penge. There were never any fish there but I liked to cool my feet and I would sometimes go there for lunch with a picnic, remembering all the fun I had had with my mates Lenny and Darren there.

There was the time Lenny's father had come by with his walking stick and threatened to slap Lenny if he didn't come home this instant! We never forgot that one.

Sometimes I'd take Mango there - he loved it. He could splash about all day and when it was time to go back, I'd have to chase him down the stream with him jumping up and down while I put on his leash. He would give me his 'puppy eyes,' sad the fun was over.

One of those days down by the stream I heard the army for the first time. The parade marched into the street and everyone stopped what they were doing. Men from Penge were off to war. I spotted Father marching in front of all of them, his collection of medals gleaming.

He had never told us there would be a parade that day. Mango ran over and snapped at the marching soldiers and I had to run over and pull him away. When I finally got Mango home, I rushed back to see the parade on my own, but it was long gone and so I huffed at Mango for the rest of the day.

'Jolly good weather, eh, chap?' Harley told me the next morning whilst I stumbled into the room.

'Eh?' I said, startled.

'Damn that Fritz,' Harley said in a put-on posh accent. 'What've they done?' he cried. 'I'll tell you what they've done. Those damn Fritz have invaded Belgium and now France.'

'But we're not in Belgium or France,' I told him.

'Think of those people, Alf,' Harley told me. 'Those brave lads in France who are-'

'About to die in those miserable trenches of theirs,' Fred finished for him as he entered the room.

I snorted and tucked into my breakfast of beans on toast.

'As I was saying,' Harley resumed his speech, putting on his poshest voice again. 'Those brave lads who are fighting the Boche for King and Country!'

'Just so you know Harley,' Fred told him, 'They're not saints. They want a life of war. Unlike me, I want a life of peace.'

'You want a life without Mother kicking you out of bed,' Harley told him. 'And laziness.'

I smirked whilst I stuffed a piece of my bread and several beans into my mouth. I loved watching those two bickering.

Harley called Fred 'Mr Bed-sticker' as it sometimes seemed like he was glued to his bed.

Fred called Harley 'Mr Action-packed' as he was to obviously sign up sooner or later and loved adventure.

Harley coughed into a handkerchief he had drawn out of his pocket and folded it up, ignoring the looks of disgust from Fred who said, 'Practising to see someone are you?' he asked. 'You're acting like you're going to meet the bloody king!'

'I'll have you know that swearing in my presence is a sign of disobedience and I shall inform Lord Kitchener immediately. I am going to meet him right now.'

'Lord Kitchener, eh?' Father piped up as he strolled into the kitchen. 'The brigadier is visiting his headquarters to talk about training and where to move the brigade when they're ready.'

'What are you doing then?' Harley asked him.

'I'm in charge of the brigade for the day. I'm going to catch the train to the training camp to see their progress.'

'Can I come?' Harley asked, immediately.

'No,' Father answered shortly.

That brought an end to the conversation.

Tension

Supper was the only time the whole family was together because Father was at the army recruiting for lunch and Fred was away doing his duties as a postman. This left Mother, Harley and me in the house, and even I tried to avoid it sometimes by taking Mango on long walks to the beach. It took a while to get there but I loved the spray of the sea on my face. So did Mango. Mother was always doing housework to keep her mind busy. Harley was always reading a book. Mostly thick books about quests.

One night, it was five o'clock in the evening and Father still wasn't back from recruiting. Eventually, after about half an hour, he pushed open the door and burst in, panting.

'Sorry I'm late,' he apologised. 'There were quite a few recruits and we were told that we needed to make a plan of action to take some weight off the French.' He broke off. Mother looked worried.

'Ned,' she said. 'You can't carry on like this. The deeper we get into this war, the harder they're going to work you. And you're nearly fifty for God's sake. Take a bit of pity on yourself.'

Father shook his head. He wasn't annoyed, he was just tired of answering this question. 'Rachel,' he explained. 'How many times have I told you? They aren't working me too hard, and as colonel I've got to be a bit more responsible than the others.' It wasn't a proper argument, just angry talk. Mother looked speechless for a moment before storming out of the room. Father sat down.

'She'll calm down,' he said. 'Once this war gets worse, she'll see that more people are needed to fight.' I didn't think so. But I hoped that it would get better before I had to leave.

We started cooking supper; boiled eggs with potatoes and carrots. Mother didn't come down. Even when supper was ready, she still wouldn't come down. Harley seemed in a mood as he stabbed down at his potatoes.

'What's wrong,' Father asked.

'It's Brian and Stephen,' Harley replied, sourly. 'All they ever talk about is the war.'

'Tell me about it,' Fred agreed. 'About ninety-five percent of the newspapers I deliver are the ones that are guaranteed to have something about the war on the front page. I mean I can't complain since I read all the articles about the war at the moment, but if I could complain, I would.'

'I haven't seen Darren and Lenny in days,' I chipped in. 'Darren, I have no idea what he's doing. Probably what you're doing, Fred. Scrounging for good news.'

For a moment everyone carried on eating. Father, it appeared, was ravenous and wolfed down his supper.

'Have we got any more eggs,' he asked.

'No,' Harley answered. 'Mango got into the coop last night. These are the only ones we have left.'

'Curse that dog,' Father grumbled. 'I'm starving.'

'We might have a few slices of bread,' I told him. Father went over to the counter. There were two slices left. He grabbed one slice and stuffed it into his mouth.

'Thanks, Alf,' he said, his mouth stuffed with bread. I ignored him and carried on eating my supper. Mango came in whining. There was a knock on the door.

'Whoever could that be,' Harley asked. I shrugged and went to answer it.

It was the army! A stern looking man was standing at the front of a group of about ten people. He had a black moustache and a hard looking face. There was a revolver in his coat pocket. He was smoking a cigarette.

'Hello, sir,' I said nervously. 'Is something the matter?'

The man drew a long breath on his cigarette before answering.

'Yes,' he said. 'Something is the matter. How old are you?' he snapped suddenly.

'Er, seventeen,' I stuttered, a little startled by his behaviour.

'Well,' the Sergeant prompted.

'Well, what?' I asked, not trying to be rude.

'Why aren't you out there fighting for King and Country?!' he exclaimed.

I was a little bewildered by this.

'Do I have to, sir?' I asked. 'I wasn't aware it was the law.'

'Of course it isn't, boy!' the sergeant cried.

'Then why do I have to be fighting?'

'It's your patriotic duty, you ruffian,' he shouted.

'Alfie,' Father had come out to see what all the kerfuffle was about. He spotted the soldiers standing outside. 'Evening, officers,' Father said. 'What brings you knocking on people's doors on this unusually quiet evening.'

'This young man hasn't registered and I was ordered to make sure everyone signs up,' the sergeant replied. He didn't seem pleased to see Father.

'Yes, well Alfie is absolutely right about what he said, er, what was your name again? Oh yes. Sergeant Kennedy,' Father said. 'He shan't sign up unless he has to or would like too. Now good day.'

'I'm afraid, sir,' the sergeant said, obviously shocked by Father's reaction, 'that is not possible.' 'Oh, is it not, sergeant,' said Father, obviously annoyed by the sergeant's stubbornness. Fred and Harley had now come down to see what was going on. 'I've worked in the army for about fifteen years. And I've earned just about every medal you can earn for a colonel.' He took off two of his best medals. One of them was the Albert medal. The sergeant recoiled with a look of shock. He stood there for a moment, turned on his heels and marched off without another word said.

'Well,' Father said. 'That's that. Of course you won't sign up unless you want to.' He went back in the house, leaving Fred, Harley and me standing there.

'I'm surprised Father didn't go and get the gun the way he looked,' Fred said.

'I know,' Harley agreed. 'I hope your sergeant isn't like that.

'I hope I'll be able to become a sergeant or something like that,' said Fred. I retreated inside the house. Father was sitting on the rocking chair, smoking his pipe. He seemed amused by the events that had just happened, muttering to himself, then shaking his head. Mother came downstairs.

'Ned?' she said. 'What just happened there. It sounded a bit like an argument.'

'Oh everything's fine, Rachel,' Father said. 'Just a squad of army men who were off their rocker. Thought the lads had to sign up,' Father explained. 'As if,' he added. 'Alfie stood up to them. Good lad. Then I told them to get out of here.' I collapsed onto the armchair. Couldn't there be some peace around here?

A few days later, I awoke to an unusually bright morning. Father was already away at work, as usual. Fred was going to sleep until mother pricked him with her knitting needles. Harley was probably already downstairs making breakfast with Mother. He had taken on lots of responsibility since he had heard we were going to go to war.

'Alfie! Fred!' Mother called. 'Breakfast.' Fred groaned. 'Just five more minutes?'

'Alright,' Mother said. 'If you want it to go cold then be my guest.'

Fred and I groaned in unison before wrenching the blanket off us. At least I did. I pulled a shirt over my head, then began stumbling down the stairs, still half asleep. Fred on the other hand had simply turned over and gone straight back to sleep. When I entered the kitchen, I was glad I had come down. Mother and Harley had produced a huge breakfast. Baked beans, sausages, some bacon and black pudding. There were about two baskets full of buns. There was a pot of jam and butter next to it. There was a pot of tea steaming by the stove.

'Hope you enjoy it,' Harley grinned. 'They were all out of eggs at the shop and we don't have any here.' I was stunned. Mother smiled.

'At least someone came downstairs,' she said. 'I'll have to wake Fred up later.' But I was already eating. By the time I was finished Fred still wasn't downstairs. 'That boy,' Mother grumbled. Every weekend or day when he knows he hasn't got anything on he just sleeps and sleeps until I drag him out of bed.' She stomped up the stairs. 'That's it young man,' she said, loudly. 'Sleepy time's over!'

'What!' Fred exclaimed. Harley and I couldn't stop a grin creeping across our mouth.

'This is my favourite bit,' Harley said. I nodded. 'Let's go see what's happening in the flesh,' Harley said. We crept into the hallway. Then we snuck up the stairs.

'Mother?' Fred said. 'I was sleeping. You can't just wake me up. It's good to wake up naturally.'

'It is your last day in this place for a very long time so you will spend it with family, and you will spend it out of your bed.' I was confused. Last day in this place? What did she mean? Fred seemed dazed for a moment before slumping onto his pillow. Mother pulled him to his feet, opened his wardrobe and threw a shirt and some trousers at him. 'I expect you down there in five minutes.' She stomped back down the stairs. Slowly Fred dragged on his clothes. There were newspapers all over his bed, pages strewn on the floor. I looked at one of the headlines.

Devonport Naval Base Attacked By Germans

'Why would anyone attack Devonport?' I asked Fred.

'God knows why,' he replied. 'I've heard of some stupid stuff before, but that has got to be one of the stupidest things I ever heard of.'

'I mean, it's one of the biggest naval ports in the country,' I said. 'Surely they'd be armed to the teeth.'

'That's the stupid thing about it,' Fred agreed. But we fought them off. They still made their mark. A couple of ships were damaged; destroyed their engines I think. There was a small fire in one of the ship's boiler rooms. One stoker nearly lost a leg from the fire but otherwise there weren't any injuries or deaths. They did capture some Germans. They said they'd interrogate them. Poor folks.' He pointed to his poster board covered with photographs. 'Here's their picture.'

Underneath were three men with mournful expressions. Their wrists were cuffed in front of them, and an Admiral stood behind them with a proud look on his face.

'Maybe they'll get something out of them,' Harley said, hopefully. 'I mean there's no way the Germans will already be planning an attack on London soon. At least not a full scale one. They'd need resources for that and the war has only been going for about a week or two.'

I looked at the date of the newspaper. It was dated yesterday.

'Fred?' Harley asked. 'What did Mother mean when she said it was your last day in this place?'

'She meant that it was basically my last day in this place,' Fred replied glumly.

'You don't say,' Harley gasped. Before Fred could say anything Harley was rifling through his wardrobe.

Suddenly, he stopped in his tracks then pulled out a spotless khaki-coloured cap with the Queen's Own Royal West Kent Regiment badge.

'You did,' Harley whispered. I was confused. Then I put one-and-one together: Fred had joined up.

'It wasn't my choice,' Fred protested.

'What happened?' Harley asked.

So Fred told us. Apparently, Father had talked it over with Mother; Mother had disagreed, but Father was adamant: Fred would have to sign up. He was the oldest and Father was an army officer. There was nothing else for it.

They had put him down as a reserve and he would have to leave in a few days.

That decided it for Harley and I. We were signing up too.

'Frederick!' Mother shouted. 'Get out of bed for Heaven's sake.'

Fred nearly jumped out of his skin with fright. He hadn't even started getting dressed. Now if there was anything Fred was good at it was getting dressed in under a minute. His hands flew from button to button and in no time he did up the final button on his waistcoat. He trotted down the stairs. It was a sunny day so I fancied taking a stroll in the streets. I'd probably end up walking by the town hall. I always did. Lots of the paths I liked lead to it.

'Mother,' I said. 'I'm going for a walk.'

Off To War

The first thing I noticed in the morning was Fred's uniform. It was spotless and his cap badge had been polished.

I laid down the knives and forks, noticing that Mother was pursing her lips.

'You're going today, aren't you,' I guessed.

Fred nodded.

'I'm coming with you,' Harley said instantly.

'No, you're not,' Father told him. 'You're staying here until you're seventeen.'

'Ever heard of the Marne?' Fred said, referring to a battle in which the British has just lost thousands of men.

'Yeah,' Harley said, 'we won.'

'By a smidge.'

'And a smidge is enough to get a foothold.'

'Shut up,' Fred yawned, accepting his mug of tea from Mother as she swooped by and taking a deep gulp before realising it was too hot.

'I'm going,' Harley said firmly.

'No, you aren't,' Mother told him.

'Rachel…' Father reasoned with her. 'If he's desperate to go, then he should. He has been dreaming about it since he was old enough to understand.'

'Well, he's far too young and shall have to wait until he's old enough.'

'You just don't want to be lonely,' Harley told her. 'I'll sign up by myself then.'

Mother pursed her lips but didn't say anything.

That took the decision out of my hands; I would have to sign up with Harley and Fred.

I trudged down the path with Fred and Harley, looking for the recruiting office. 'They said it was near the town center,' Fred told us.

Harley nodded and looked down the street at the town school where I saw the children having their break. Two of them were rolling around, cursing and kicking, whilst the others chanted, 'Fight! Fight! Fight!'

Eventually, the headmaster came and hauled them into the school building where I heard the forbidding crack of the cane. We joined the queue leading into the recruiting office where we waited to be let in. When it came to me, I stepped into the building where the recruiting sergeant was waiting, his pen poised over a form.

'Name?' he asked.

'Alfred Tuck,' I replied, wincing at my real name.

'Date of birth?'

'March 14th 1897.'

'Occupation?'

'Mechanic.'

He scribbled my name and date of birth on a form and handed it to me.

'Move on,' the recruiting sergeant told me.

I moved on to a station where a doctor was standing.

'Cough,' he said. I coughed. 'Fit as a fiddle,' he said. 'Stand here.' He pointed to a ruler stick with a bar at the bottom. 'Stand straight.'

I stood straight as he lifted the bar to my head. 'Five foot six,' he said.

'Go straight on,' he told me. 'They'll give you your uniforms when you get there.'

I waited for Fred and Harley. When they emerged, Fred's mood had sunk more, but Harley looked delighted. He had fooled the recruiters about his age and it didn't sound like it took too much effort. We left for the local train station.

Finally, after an enjoyable hour on the train – with plenty of laughter -- we arrived at our destination.

The training camp stretched for about two miles along the woods. There were several hundred tents with two beds in each. We reported to the lieutenant-colonel's office where he was sorting through his files. He looked up when we entered.

'Names?' he asked.

'Tuck.'

'OK, you three,' he told us. 'You're now under my command and as I understand you're my commanding officer's sons.'

We nodded.

'Well, no matter who you are in the brigade, you're just a normal private in my battalion, understand? Good. Now, you'll be learning that you do as I, or one of your officers, say. Otherwise, it'll be punishment and chores - which usually take a good few hours - so just pay attention. Dismissed.'

I took a tent with Harley and dumped my kit on my bed. I laid back and tried to relax for a moment. I had barely laid down for five minutes when I heard a bell. I looked out of the tent and spotted a figure walking down the row of tents.

'Do you know who I am?' he shouted at us. 'Well, I'm your sergeant, that's who I am.'

He walked straight up to me and I recognised him. It was Sergeant Kennedy, the one who had come by the house, demanding we sign up. 'And as I'm your sergeant you'd better do as I say. And I say if your kit isn't thundering shiny within the hour then you'll be sorry for it. And when I mean shiny, I mean so shiny that you can see every spot on your face in the reflection. And if your rifle isn't sparkling either then you'll be in trouble too.' He looked each one of us in the face and bellowed, 'Well get on with it!'

We scarpered off into our tents and started cleaning our kit.

'Alfie,' Harley said. 'Remember your rucksack and the kit inside. That sergeant's going to want that spick and span too.'

I nodded and unpacked the rucksack the sergeant had given me. Inside it was a water flask, a few tins of food, a trench digging shovel, and a field medical kit. A roll that looked a bit like a mattress or something and a sheath with a bayonet in it. I strapped the sheath with the bayonet to my side and started cleaning with a cloth that was included in the kit.

I polished buttons and buckles, cleaned the barrel of my rifle, and scrubbed the bayonet with a drop of oil so that it wouldn't get rusty.

When that hour was up, I had finished cleaning my kit and was ordered into a line of two columns, our rucksacks and its contents laid in front of us. We stood behind the kit, bolt upright, waiting for approval.

From that moment on our days were spent on kit inspection, eating meals, crawling up hills on our stomachs, learning how to use various weapons such as grenades and rifles, digging trenches, practising marching in time with the rest swinging your arms and legs in time to 'one two three four'.

We got up at five o'clock in the morning to the sound of a bell or trumpet. First, we had kit inspection, then breakfast. We'd then do drills around the parade for a couple of hours; marching, turning, marching, turning. After lunch we'd either have a small rest then be back to drills or combat training. We learnt how to load, aim and fire a rifle; and how to thrust a bayonet. Once we were ordered to crawl through a field and fire at dummies at the bottom of the hill. Then we had to run over the dummies and plunge our bayonets into them. 'Jab, twist, out,' the sergeants and corporals bellowed. 'Jab, twist, out.'

For about three months we believed the war was distant, and it would be over soon. But over time stories of all the casualties in France filtered through the camp and we knew it wouldn't be as easy as we had thought. Our bodies were already sore and now our good cheer was starting to fade a little too.

In the little free time I had, I cleaned my uniform or wrote a letter to Mother. I would tell her that it was fine at the camp and we were going to be moved to France soon. Her letters were always full of encouragement, saying that she hoped I would come home soon. She had once sent me a newspaper cutting of a dogfight. You could see that the planes weren't Allies as there were flashes of light between them that resembled machine gun fire. I remember replying to all of those letters immediately, writing about everything we had done that day, and how grand I looked in a uniform, and that I was stronger than I had been and more sophisticated.

Then one day we set off to France. We all climbed onto a ship and were soon greeted by tremendous waves that sent it turning with every bump. I vomited all my sea sickness out of me and retreated from the deck. I didn't seem to be the only one who was having trouble with the sea. I had seen the sea before but never been on a boat that felt like it was sinking. The officers simply went into their cabins and read a book or smoked a cigarette. The sea didn't seem to bother them too much.

It took hours for us to reach France and by then many of the soldiers were too sick to even stand up straight.

Waiting for us were about five hundred men bent double, their eyes and faces gaunt, and bandages wrapped around them. They were shivering.

'G'luck, lads,' one of the soldiers called out. 'Give 'em a run for their money.' I gulped and looked ahead.

We arrived at the camp in the dark and went straight to our tents. I was exhausted but I was also worried. I could hear the guns rumbling in the distance, pounding each other to a standstill. I lay on my bunk and started to drift off, Harley's snores comforting me. And yet I was too anxious to properly fall asleep. I knew what those men on the front line were going through was unimaginable for me right now. And I knew that's where I was heading too. The morning seemed like it would never come. It was only sheer exhaustion that finally let my mind switch off for a few hours.

The Real Deal

As we marched on we passed other units, French or British but none stopped marching. They were all too exhausted, too injured, too shell shocked. This was when I realised it. This wasn't training. This wasn't training, knowing you're going to survive. This was knowing that one day a bullet or a shell will strike you down. This was the real deal.

For supper I had an unusually tasty pheasant. I had shot it and shared it with some others. The distant sound of artillery fire chorused in the distance. I couldn't tell if they were our guns or German guns.

Weeks passed and we didn't come into contact with the Germans. We had now entered a line of trenches on Germany's so-called 'Western Front'. As we were not experienced we had been put in the support trench for a couple of weeks before moving to a sector on the front line.

As I found out it wasn't so much terror as boredom in the trenches as there was nothing to do.

I spent most of the day waiting or trying to catch up on some sleep.

There were occasional raids and sniper duels, and sometimes artillery bombardments, but other than that it was plain boredom.

I would occasionally hollow a small section into a side of a trench and shelter, but there was never time for that as I would have to be sent on missions such as fetching supplies from the reserve trench, setting up machine guns, building or digging dugouts, mending and digging trenches.

Our battalion's trench stretched as far as the eye could see, and there were always platoons or sections marching through the communication trenches, filling in spaces of missing units returning from their time in the other trenches.

Signs had been put up further down the lines such as:

BEANS FOR FIVE BOB

And further down the line there would be signs such as:

KEEP YOUR HEAD DOWN
DON'T LOOK UP
IT MAY BE THE LAST THING YOU DO

Of course, we knew not to look above the trenches so we were always hunched.

Our trenches were gradually widening to a couple of meters, giving us space to lie down.

Sometimes when the rain wouldn't be so hard I would write letters to Mother telling her about how it was and that we were fine. When she replied I would always read her letter repeatedly.

Periscopes, and rifles were leaning against the sandbags in the trenches. There were machine guns at the top of the trenches. The mood was grim. Some soldiers were lying down, their caps over their eyes sleeping. Others were talking darkly. There were rats everywhere, scuttling around, nibbling at mouldy crusts of bread. The officers were usually in their dugouts. I just sat around and shivered.

After two weeks the hope I had was fading. The battlefield between us and the Germans was full of landmines and reams of barbed wire. Small groups had been sent on raids but few or none returned. I knew there was going to be an attack soon. One side or the other would attack.

One night, shells missed our trenches by meters. I could feel the ground shudder and the earth explode. The Germans never did come over though. And soon enough I found out why. We had an extra machine gun post positioned so perfectly that if the Germans did try anything, they would be gunned down.

But one day bad news came. The Germans had captured our machine gun post. They would be able to attack whenever they pleased.

'Who do you reckon will attack first?' Lenny asked one night. 'Got to be us, right. I hope it is.'

He was right.

One morning in March, it was time. Soldiers were putting up ladders all along the line. At around seven thirty, the whistle blew. I climbed up my ladder and charged out of the trench. Machine guns blasted, gunning many down. Mines exploded, leaving holes and piles of earth in which you could take cover. I leaped behind a mound of dirt. I loaded a clip into the magazine and fired. I ran forwards, a new sort of sheer determination leading me on. We reached the barbed wire between the two fronts. There were a few gaps in it, allowing us to slip through. I hid behind a pile of sandbags, waiting for the coast to be clear. I pulled out a grenade. Fumbling with the pin, I pulled it out and chucked it into the trench. There was a huge explosion and I jumped into the trench. There was no one there.

And then the Germans struck. They had left their trenches empty and now charged back towards us. We realised we had been tricked and retreated in a panic. Bullets missed me by inches. Shells exploded. I dived into a shell hole, splashing into a puddle. I crawled back out on my stomach. I pressed the rifle to my eye, searching for a German. I spotted one and fired at him. He fell backwards and I knew I had hit him. Now our battalion was pushing forward again.

I ran forward reaching for another grenade, only to suddenly realise our battalion was retreating yet again.

It was all over in a flash, without me ever really figuring out whether we were coming or going. We had had many casualties, so many lying out there in no man's land. That was my first experience of true war.

Several days later, our battalion found itself in the reserve trench, recovering from our first battle. There was no fighting at all there but lots of drills and inspections. I found it hard to watch new troops entering the trenches. They had no idea what they were in for.

Sometime in April, when we were back at the front, I heard a terrible rumour that the Germans had used a poisonous gas and had driven a whole army out of their trenches, killing the ones who couldn't get away quickly enough. I prayed they would not use it on us. But, of course, you cannot have everything you want in this world.

Daily life in the trenches was actually quite boring, so officers gave us jobs like sentry duty or fixing the trenches. I'd sometimes hear the cry of soldiers going over the top and hear machine gun fire of the whistle of shells and whizzbangs from the Germans.

There hadn't been much fighting since our first battle. But that was all to change. The next week I heard that we would be moving to Festubert in France to assist Indian and fellow British troops. We were all meant to attack alongside the French who trying to take a place called Vimy Ridge.

'We're going to Festubert and I'm jolly well happy,' Lenny sang, 'We're going to Festubert and ...'

'Shut up will you,' Darren scolded. 'I don't even want to go to Festubert and now we're going to march into a fully-fledged battle. It's not gonna be like training or that attack we did. It's gonna be a battle that might go on for a month.' Lenny stopped prancing around. He opened his mouth to retort.

'Quit it,' I said. 'We're going to Festubert and that's that.' I got up and put my cap on. 'I'm going for my food ration. Unless you don't want supper.' Lenny groaned.

'What?'

'What do you reckon it is today?' Lenny asked. 'Pea soup or Bully Beef? Why couldn't they make things we actually like. Pea soup is great and all but after two months of it I'd rather sprouts.' I pulled Lenny to his feet and went to the rationing table.

'Five bob for a double ration,' one of the cooks cried.

'As if,' Lenny scoffed. 'Nobody's even got five bob.' We took our ration and sat by a machine-gunning position. I took out a map and studied it.

'Festubert is ages away,' I moaned. Lenny peered into no man's land. A shot rang out. 'For Christ's sake, Lenny,' I said as we ducked down. 'What the hell are you doing looking into no man's land?'

It took us three long days of marching to get to Festubert. Lieutenant-Colonel Frenner said that we would be attacking on the fifteenth of May which was in three days. Once we got there, I laid out a row of barbed wire and set up other obstacles which were ordered to do. At night all you could hear was the growling of gunfire, knowing that your enemy was only five hundred meters away. At eight in the morning German artillery opened fire on us. Men were blasted out of their trenches, several at a time. For two days shells rained down upon us. The day before we were going to attack we were called to Father's dugout.

'At seven forty our forces are going to attack,' Father said. 'You are going to attack the German front line. When you climb out they will still be shelling you, but if you move quickly you won't get hit. First one in that trench gets double ration for the rest of the battle. And don't stay in those trenches long because our artillery is going to shell it five minutes after the battle. Good luck.' And with that we were dismissed to be with our thoughts for the rest of the day.

'I'm starting to think I should have become a combat medic. At least you only have to come after the battle,' Fred mumbled. I agreed and went off to a spot near the captain's dugout. They were studying a map of the battlefield.

'Oh,' Captain Miltain said. 'Hello Private.' I saluted. I looked more closely at the map. It had three colours on it. I recognised the flag four centimeters away from us.

'India?' I said in astonishment. Captain Miltain and his comrades began shuffling other troops around the battlefield.

'The rest of our troops. There is a backup battalion and two other battalions, flanking us on either side. The Indians are more supporting troops. Now don't you have more to do, Private?' I saluted then exited the dugout.

'What the hell are you doing in Cap'n's dugout,' came a voice behind me. I spun around. A drunk soldier was standing there with a sneer on his face. 'Get lost ya filthy cockroach,' he shouted. He then swung a punch at me.

'Oi,' Fred had appeared. 'What's you doing to my brother.' The drunk soldier sneered again and then lashed out at Fred. All of a sudden, they were rolling around in the dirt beating each other up, swearing in between the thumps. The drunk man managed to pin Fred to a sandbag and drew his bayonet threateningly. I leaped at him, managing to push him over. Another soldier fired a shot in the air.

'Stop it!' he yelled. There was always fighting in the trenches, but this was the first time a shot had been fired. I slammed the butt of my rifle into the drunk man's knee. As if things couldn't get any worse, another soldier joined the fight. He lunged at me, squeezing my throat. I reached for a trench raiding club which was only a few inches away. The soldier saw what I was doing and slammed me onto the floor.

'Break it up, break it up,' a voice yelled. I kicked back, but only felt air. Sergeant Kennedy had dragged the soldier off me. 'What the hell are you doing,' he bellowed. 'Stop fighting yourselves and fight the enemy. And since you've been so kind to try and break Tuck's back, maybe you can go into no man's land armed with a club. You too, Seline,' he shouted at the drunk man. 'Tucks, get yourselves to the dressing station. And don't you worry, you're on sentry duty for a week.' I groaned. Fred and I trudged towards the dressing station. I had a black eye and a proper nosebleed. Fred had a long cut from the bayonet.

'What have you two been doing?' an astounded medic asked. 'Shouldn't you be fighting the enemy? Never mind.

Best get you patched up.' Once we were done, I trudged to a quiet corner in the trenches and closed my eyes.

'Get up,' Major Bennet roared. 'Get up. Unless you want to be left behind. The battle of Festubert starts in five minutes.' I glanced at my watch. So it would. It was seven thirty-five. 'Get to your positions!' A shell exploded blasting six men straight out of the trench. 'On your ladders!' The whistle blew. The battle of Festubert had begun. Shells rained down upon us. A lance corporal diagonally in front of me stepped on a landmine. The force blew me back several yards. I got up and carried on running. I crouched down along a line of barbed wire. I dived through a gap, just in time before several other soldiers who had followed me were gunned down. I spotted a trench raiding club lying in the middle of a ditch. Next to it was the drunk man, three bullet wounds in his leg. I rushed over to him.

'Mate,' he said weakly. 'Leave me here. I ain't got nothing.' I shook my head and lifted him up. I carried him to a shell hole and laid him there. 'You'll be alright,' I promised. 'Here.' I handed him my bayonet. 'Now you're safe.' I charged back into the battlefield and followed my fellow soldiers towards the trenches. I crouched behind a tree stump and aimed. Machine gun bullets missed me by inches. I aimed at the machine gunner who was firing at me. Just for a moment I could see the whites of his eyes.

'Private!' Sergeant Kennedy rushed towards me. 'Fire for god's sake.' The machine gunner fired a short burst at his legs. He missed. 'You bastard,' Sergeant Kennedy roared. He fired his revolver at his chest. He hit him. 'That'll teach him,' he muttered, running over to him. 'When you see those imbeciles, you aim your rifle and you shoot them dead.' I dashed towards the trench. Dying trees were alight everywhere. I was still about fifty yards from the enemy. Other men were already at their final line of wire. I caught up with the rest of the soldiers. We would never have made it into their trench, if our artillery hadn't started firing early. Mortar shells were blowing up enemy trenches. I was thrown back from the blast and landed on a pile of destroyed wire. The next thing I recalled was other soldiers running away, following explosions and a medic rushing up to me from behind.

'Is he going to be alright, sir?' a voice asked. I tried to open my eyes but found that it was difficult. 'I don't know, Private,' a voice replied. 'He's got a fragment of rusted barbed wire in his back. A part of his spine has been chipped, and he's swallowed a breath of gas. He's been unconscious for three days and been drifting in and out for another three.' I groaned. My vision was blurred, but I could make out a doctor standing by my bed, and a crowd of visitors standing by the doorway. The doctor spun around.

'Tuck!' he exclaimed. 'You're awake.' He gave me a glass of water.

'Alfie,' Fred was among the visitors. 'How are you?' I grimaced then realised I had a cast around my head.

'What happened?' I asked. Fred opened his mouth but was interrupted.

'We all got pretty bashed up and it's all the artillery's fault,' said the man I had rescued. 'The name's Tom,' he said. He already knew my name. 'I've stopped drinking so heavily,' he said.

'You still owe me a bayonet,' I said, smiling. 'Anyway, how long was I unconscious for?' I asked.

'About six days,' said Harley, who also appeared to be among the visitors. 'The battle's nearly over. One more fight and they say this'll be done. Of course, they're wrong. Anyway. They say we only got to see you for a few minutes.' And then they all went. Then Father came in.

'What you did out there Alfie,' he said. 'That was really good. I've got a little present for you.' He pressed something cold into the palm of my hand. He then left. The doctor ordered a nurse to run a few tests on me. She was a nice lady, about my age, with long hair, the colour of caramel chocolate that Cadbury's make. Her kind blue eyes had a sympathy in them, and her face was as good as anyone's.

After a few days, I began to grow fond of her and started looking forward to the hours when she would run her soft, tender hands along my forehead to check if I had a temperature, when she would make a cool drink or just wrap a new bandage round my head. I think maybe she began to grow fond of me too, because the day I left for the front line again, she gave me a brisk kiss on the cheek and went off to do her nursing duties.

We had won the battle of Festubert and we were about fifteen miles further away than we had been when I was injured. I had been in hospital for three months and had grown used to the good food, good care and as many good things you could think of. I had received several letters from Mother, Fred and Harley. They read like this:

Dearest Alfie,

I have heard that you were injured in battle and that it was barbed wire and an explosion that injured you. I hope they are treating you correctly at the hospital and you are recovering. It is in the papers that you won the battle of Festubert and your name is among the list of wounded. I would like to know a bit more detail of how exactly you got this injury of yours. They never are clear about these things in the newspapers. Your name is also among those who were awarded a medal, about which I am most proud of you for. It says you got the Albert Medal, that's quite something. Mango misses you all most terribly and sticks to standing by the gate waiting for you until I take him in. We are missing you most terribly and hope that you will come home soon.

Your loving Mother

Dear Alfie,

How's the head? The trenches are worse than ever and a lot of soldiers are suffering with trench foot. I hope you are enjoying yourself at the hospital. Another batch of newbies came into the trenches in their spotless uniforms and everyone asked them how good the baths were back in Blighty. They were obviously shocked at how we love baths nowadays. We are marching towards Belgium and might go there. Kennedy was killed a couple of days ago, shame that. He saved you from breaking your back in that fight. I hope your wounds aren't too bad because when you get here you're going to wish you were ill. We haven't been in too many fights since May but are short of food and they've got to feed about three thousand men. I'm good and so is Fred. See you soon.
                                    Harley

Dear Alfie,

Your Royal West Kent regiment isn't doing too well. Loads more are getting diseased and trying to desert. Your mates Lenny and Darren are worried sick about you, as am I. They say they will never rely on our artillery again. I just want this war to be over. And oh, don't go losing your head over that girl you like at the hospital. You're probably never going to see her again. It seems ages ago that you became eighteen and you're soon going to be a Lance

Corporal. Sonny says "Me mum would murder me if I fell on barbed wire." I wouldn't argue with him. He's always right somehow. Make it back safely. But when you do get here; remember to hide your food as the rats are bigger than ever.

Fred

A Bit of This. A Bit of That.

Fred was right. The rats were huge. Unfortunately, the same could not be said for the soldiers. We had been promised victory but we were not succeeding at all. I was happy that they had equipped us with gas masks after the disaster at the battle of Ypres where the Germans killed more than two thousand French troops with their poison gas. The gunfire was less and less frequent until finally it stopped for days on end. Some days groups of enemy soldiers would sneak into our trenches and attempt to sabotage our line. One day, they came so close to planting a mine near Father's dugout that his assistants were immediately replaced. Another, I was cleaning my rifle when I heard a cry.

'Gas. Gas. There's bloody gas floating over no man's land.'

There was immediate panic. We fumbled with our gas masks. All of a sudden, a shell exploded in our trench. I fixed my bayonet to the end of my rifle and looked up into no man's land. There it was. The gas hung in the air, reaching its way across the battlefield, its long tentacles wrapping themselves around everything in their path.

'Bloody hell,' I screamed. 'It's coming.' Shells continued to rain down upon us. I ran to the nearest dugout where half a dozen men were cowering.

'It's in the trenches. The gas is in the blimmin' trenches.' Ignoring the shells, we evacuated the trench. We escaped to our support trench where half our soldiers were stumbling struggling to see. We managed to avert the worst, but many of our best men had been blinded. We carried them out onto fields where they were tended to by field medics.

By mid-September things were getting peaceful again. But one night there was a huge assault launched on our field hospital by the Germans' best combat veterans. I was eating my pea soup beside a small fire when someone came running down the trenches. 'Sir! Sir! A telephone call came in from the field. It's under attack. The hospital.' Father spun around. He whispered something to Captain Miltain.

'C battalion is to help our medics,' he ordered. 'This will be led by Captain Miltain. Go!' Captain Miltain shepherded our battalion off to the field hospital. I could hear rifle fire and knew that if we didn't get there soon it would be overrun. Finally, we spotted the Germans.

'Charge,' yelled Captain Miltain. We charged firing furiously at the Germans. I hid behind a pile of boxes. We had barely enough time to fit our bayonets onto the end of our gun. I fired until I ran out of ammunition. I spotted a wounded lance corporal lying on the floor, soaked in blood.

'Private,' he gasped. I could see a wound right in his chest. I didn't know much about medical stuff but I did know that you have to clean a wound. I tore off a bit of my uniform, poured some water on it and dabbed it at his wound. Then I handed it to him. 'Keep on doing that.' He nodded vaguely. 'Lecrindo. Lance Corporal Lecrindo. Tell them that you saved Lance Corporal Lecrindo's life.' I nodded. I picked up my empty rifle and handed it to him. I picked up his rifle and gestured. 'May I?' He nodded. I then ran off. It turns out Lance Corporal Lecrindo had not fired any shots before he was hit.

The battle raged on all night. I restocked on ammunition by taking from the wounded. I was exhausted, but we kept on battering each other. In the dark, I ran towards a body lying face down in the dirt. I turned it over. It was Sonny, our friend from home. His short hair was smothered with blood. I noticed wounds on his leg and head. Somehow, he was still breathing. I picked him up over my shoulder and bent low, carrying him all the way to the trenches.

'Oh, Lord,' a medic cursed. 'This one's been sucker punched by the bastards. I'll do my best on him. Don't you worry. It's just these wounds are unlucky. Pierced his skull this one did. For sure.' I left him and returned to the field hospital, which was more like a battlefield now. Tents were on fire. As were tables and crates. I had to crawl to get anywhere without getting hit. And I couldn't do it if I was under fire. So, it was best to just stay put. But somehow more of our soldiers were pushing forward. They were finding cover and pushing back. Inch by inch, metre by metre, we were driving them away. Eventually, the German soldiers were pushed back to their trenches, battered and exhausted. As were we.

The sudden attack on our field hospital had left us in disarray. Soldiers had their wounds dressed in the boggy trenches. Sonny started making a slow recovery but could eat little and was constantly having panic attacks. The doctor said he would be of no use until he calmed down and healed so he sent him to a hospital about thirty miles behind the line.

I sat sipping my tea thinking about how this had all started from one man – a royal in a far-away land – getting shot. One man's life for thousands is a terrible cost. The year was changing into a freezing November. I had been in the army for over a year now, and I had still not been promoted. Many of the soldiers were homesick and starved. The tea was lukewarm, but it managed to warm me. Suddenly, a huge rat leaped at my mug.

'Argh,' I cried. 'Wretched blighter. Get away.' I whacked it with my rifle until it scurried off. The mug had fallen off the table and spilt the tea. 'Damn,' I cursed.

'Attention,' a voice bellowed. I stood up. The trench was jampacked. 'Any volunteers for a mission up to no man's land?' Naturally no one spoke up. 'Good. A squad is going up to no man's land to infiltrate their radio dugout. After that, change their codes and we'll be able to listen in on their telephone calls. Now go, go, go.' For a moment no one moved and then, recovering, bustled around doing their duties, hoping they wouldn't be noticed.

'Not so fast,' Major Bennet said. 'Tuck,' he said, pointing at me. 'You're in. As are you, you, and how about you, Eastwood, and you, Bowl, and who else… you.' He had selected Harley, Fred, Lenny and Darren and of course, Staff Sergeant Rought.

'Now fix bayonets. Make sure you have a full magazine and a spare clip.' We followed him as he crawled out of the trench. Instantly, machine guns chattered away at us, whizzing over our heads as we slid across no man's land. I didn't dare fire back. Staff Sergeant Rought pointed towards an empty machine-gunning post. Our support platoon fired back and soon the Germans weren't concerned about us any longer.

It turned out that the machine-gunning post was occupied. I slithered into the trench. 'Wake them,' Staff Sergeant mouthed. I prodded one of the sleeping soldiers who jerked awake, a look of alarm across their face as they realised who we were. 'Someone stay here with these scumbags,' Staff Sergeant Rought commanded. Darren disarmed them and then stayed, pointing his rifle at them in turn. The rest of us crept towards the radio dugout. 'Look over there,' a German exclaimed in German pointing at us. Staff Sergeant Rought fired at him twice. We were in trouble now. We had attracted attention. There were four men inside the dugout when we entered. Two swung their guns around at us, but were shot before they could hit us. The rest surrendered.

'Alright. Tuck. I hear you're good with this stuff. Dismantle it so we can listen in.' I nodded and started fiddling with the phone. I didn't exactly know what to do but I understood machines and I knew you just had to play around with them until you figured it out.

'Hurry up, Private,' Staff Sergeant Rought hissed. I fumbled with the last few cables then finished. I nodded to Staff Sergeant Rought and crept out of the dugout. I heard the sound of footsteps. 'Take this lot.' He nodded at the two radio coordinators. 'Prod them in the direction. One each. Eastwood take this one. Tuck,' he said. 'You,' he pointed at Fred. 'Take this one. We'll cover you from behind.'

We made it back to Darren. He was lying injured against a wall. Just as it dawned on us what had happened, several things happened at once. A series of shots rang out, and there was swearing. Lots of it. I fired three times and pulled Darren up. 'Get out. Get out now. Abort mission.' We scrambled out of the trench. I was still dragging Darren along. Personally, I was lucky I didn't get shot. I dived behind a mound of earth and prayed to God.

And then they started shelling us. Masses of explosives were uprooting trees. I moved only when half our assailants were reloading. Suddenly, a pain flared up in my right leg. I fell forward and collapsed into a puddle.

'Alfie,' Darren groaned. 'I've got a flare in my rucksack. Lieutenant Colonel Frenner equipped me with it when I went on a messaging mission. Pull it out. Use it when it's safer.' I took it in my hand. I tried to ignore the pain in my leg but found it impossible. Fred had made it into our trenches along with Lenny, Harley, and the two Germans. Staff Sergeant Rought was still fighting. Not abandoning the mission. My vision was fading fast, until I blacked out.

'Alfie!' Darren was shaking me. 'Get up. The fighting's stopped. We need to get back.' I groaned. I had no idea how much time had passed. But I struggled up. We crouched down and made our way back to our trenches.

'Alfie for god's sake, I thought you were dead.' I nodded vaguely. 'Oh my god,' Fred exclaimed. 'You're injured, but you're back.' With all the soldiers clapping around me I drifted off into unconsciousness.

'He's awake,' voices muttered. I opened my eyes. It was dawn and I was lying in a hospital bed all over again. 'How's the leg,' Fred grinned. I carefully peaked at the wound. It was a bloody mess but it had been cleaned up. 'How long have I been out for?' I asked. Harley grimaced. I knew it hadn't been that long. 'Couple of hours. You were bleeding like mad. Lance Corporal,' he added. 'Oh I forgot to tell you. You were promoted while you were out. You should great bravery out there and more than that, leadership. The General heard the news. Said you deserved it.' I nodded. I lay in bed for the rest of the day.

My leg throbbed whenever I touched it but it was patched up after a couple of days. It still wouldn't move fluently but at least it worked. In December I heard that Field Marshal Haig was making an alliance with the French so we could attack together. My leg was healing well and I was able to hobble around the perimeter of the hospital garden.

'Lance Corporal!' a voice shouted while I was doing my morning hobble around the hospital. It was Staff Sergeant Rought, with his inimitably stern tone. 'I hear you've been bunking off from the army because you've got an injury. Well, you've been in here long enough.' And suddenly, he swept my stick out from beneath me. I toppled over and landed on my face. 'Get up, Lance Corporal and show some honour. Put some effort into it.' He swept my stick away again. This time, I managed to stay on my feet for a couple of seconds. And then I fell over again.

'Staff Sergeant!' a nurse shrieked. 'Are you visiting young Alfred?' Staff Sergeant Rought was enraged.

'Yes, I am,' he retorted. 'And may I ask why he is still stuck in this hospital. He is needed at the front.'

'Well, he shall stay as long as his leg needs to recover and the fact that he is already walking again is a very good sign. And may I ask, if you are merely visiting him why is he on the floor and his stick by your feet?'

'I uh… it doesn't matter,' Staff Sergeant Rought stammered, before remembering his rank. 'I can do as I please.' And with that he marched off. The nurse I so liked scooped me up and handed me my stick. 'By the way, my name's Mara. Come on. Best get you to your bed.' I smiled and allowed myself to be steered to my bed, collapsing onto it. The covers were soft and I felt myself drifting off immediately.

I stayed in the hospital for another three months until I could walk properly and run steadily. I relaxed on my bed on the last week before I left.

'Happy Birthday to you. Happy Birthday to you. Happy Birthday dear Alfie. Happy Birthday to you.' Fred, Harley, Lenny, Tom and Mara had interrupted me and Darren (he shared the room with me as he was also injured and if you were injured on a patrol you got to stay in a special room) from eating our supper.

'We're going over to the blasted Somme in a couple of months,' Lenny exclaimed. 'Haig says that there's gonna be a huge assault and we'll have pushed Fritz back by September or something.' Darren looked astounded and winced as people sat on his bed, for his leg still hurt. The cake was uneven but it tasted wonderful all the same. I ate three. I felt healthily exhausted after that. But I was getting more exhausted.

'How do you save a man,' Lenny was saying. 'I ain't saved one yet and I've got no medals except for this one here.' He jabbed his thumb at a medal pinned to his chest. 'And no one ain't even gonna consider promoting Lenny Eastwood.' Everybody laughed. I yawned and spotting my tired expression, they left me to sleep. 'Some birthday, huh,' Darren mumbled. I nodded and, influenced by my tiredness and relief, drifted off to sleep.

'Alfie. Alfie, get up.' I opened my eyes.

'What?'

'You're in the papers.'

'So? You've been in the papers. You might still be in the papers cos of your injury.'

'Just look at it,' Darren said.

'No can do,' I teased. 'A wounded man can do as he pleases.'

'I'm a wounded man,' Darren retorted.

'I'm a wounded Lance Corporal.'

'And you're a wounded Lance Corporal with the Distinguished Conduct Medal.'

'Don't tease.'

'I'm not.'

'You are.'

'Just open your eyes and read it.'

'Fine. But I'm only reading the headline and looking at the picture.'

'What's new?' Darren snorted.

I looked at the newspaper and saw the usual list of the mounting casualties. 'Darren?' I said. 'What's interesting about names?'

'This,' he said pointing at one. I saw the name Alfred Tuck where I had been injured and what regiment I was in. Then I saw something that made me stutter.

I had never known that the Distinguished Conduct Medal was the medal I had recently won.

I flipped through the rest of the paper and saw a headline with a picture of me on it. It read:

Alfred Tuck DCM

'Looks like you're famous,' Darren chuckled.

'Wanna trade?' I said sarcastically.

'Wouldn't mind,' Darren shrugged.

'OK,' I agreed. 'Just get yourself to headquarters and ask the General and you'll be a Lance Corporal, easy.'

'Ask Harley that,' Darren said. 'He'd give anything to be ranked up.'

'Yeah,' I sighed. 'I suppose he would.'

Lance Corporal Tuck

It took some getting used to being able to command a group of about six or so soldiers. I was the only one of my friends who had been promoted and I sometimes even had a bigger ration than just regular Privates. But I didn't feel good about bossing others around. I was often chosen to command or be in a night patrol or a night raid, as I had been so successful the last time. I had even been recommended for the Victoria Cross but it had been overlooked. I didn't mind that. I was fine with the Albert Medal. I was fine being a Lance Corporal. A medal or a rank doesn't matter in a free-for-all to get across a battlefield. It will only make you more arrogant and ambitious. I was determined I would not be like that.

One day I was sitting in the trenches, thinking about how Sonny was recovering when I heard a whistle and an explosion. 'What's going on?' I asked a private who was hurrying by. He didn't answer. I heard another explosion and got up. 'They're bombing us. Get to your dugouts. Find shelter. They're firing shells.' I cowered but would not get into a shelter.

'There are wounded men blasted out of their trenches,' I shouted. 'They'll be dead when this shelling stops down.' I waited for a couple of minutes then climbed out of the trench. No one was in no man's land. The wounded were lying at the top of our trench a couple of metres away. 'Are you out of your bloody mind,' Staff Sergeant Rought roared. But he flew back as a shell exploded metres away from him. I crawled out of the trench and looked around. The nearest soldier was lying four feet away.

Rifle fire started at once but only a few whistled right by me. I crawled towards the man and rolled him over. There was blood all over his britches. I dragged him with me. He was taken down the front line.

'There's a Fritz out in no man's land!' someone yelled. I looked out and indeed there was. 'Shoot him.' But it was a trap. As soon as we showed our faces the machine guns opened up. 'Lance Corporal. Gimme a hand here.' Sergeant Lugard from the fourth battalion was trying to carry a wounded man to the field hospital. I took hold of one end of the stretcher. I made five trips to the field hospital. The shelling had eased but it still wasn't done. We were ordered to stay in the trenches. We wanted to counter attack as soon as it stopped. We stayed up all night.

'Get up the lot of you!' came an unexpected cry. 'They're coming. Get to your ladders and don't fail. Wait for the whistle.' I found a ladder and climbed up two rungs. For two minutes nothing happened. And then it came. The thing I dreaded most. The signal for us to go to no man's land. The whistle blew long and shrill, and we charged into the battlefield.

I saw the Germans about twenty metres away from their trenches. 'Find cover!' I yelled. I fired twice, hitting my target once. 'Fire!' I did what I had done at the battle near the field hospital. I took cover and fired from my cover. 'Carry on running,' Captain Miltain yelled. 'Push them back.' Other soldiers were beginning to follow him. I looked up from my position and saw that we were pushing the Germans back. I joined them. We were good at taking cover. They were good at aiming. Every time I stuck my head up I made sure I was already aiming so that I could hide within seconds. Captain Miltain hurriedly fired his revolver at the oncoming Germans.

Truth be told, it was chaos. I barely knew who was where and the smoke from the guns hung around us. Suddenly I was upon a German. Without a second's thought, I stabbed my bayonet into his gut. I saw one of their officers look over no man's land. He fired his revolver at me but missed. I replied, firing away, until he finally went down. 'Take cover,' somebody yelled.

'Gimme some help up here,' another cried. I stumbled my way across no man's land, jabbing and firing, ducking and diving. Eventually, we pushed them all the way to their trenches.

'Don't stop,' Captain Miltain yelled. As if I was in a trance I followed my battalion into their trenches. All of a sudden, flashes whizzed past me. They were hiding at the other end of their trenches and firing. 'Swing round the machine guns,' Captain Miltian ordered. I hid behind a pile of sandbags and waited for them to start up the machine guns. When they did it made little difference. I kneeled behind the sandbags and fired.

'Incoming shell! Someone yelled. We took this as our chance to push forwards. They retreated further until we couldn't see them. 'Keep pushing,' Captain Miltain yelled. 'We've got them on the run.' There were short bursts of rifle fire but the owner of it was instantly downed. I kept my rifle to my eye, checking each turn. All of a sudden, when we were about halfway through their trenches the Germans opened fire. I found a small gap in one of the trench walls and squeezed into it. Not many of us made it to cover, though. About once a minute I'd fire a shot down the trench on the off chance that I might hit somebody.

'We need a signaler,' someone shouted. 'We need a damn signaler.' I thought quickly. Maybe we could signal them with code.

'Harley,' I yelled. Please let him be alive, I prayed. Then I saw him. He was down a trench that was jammed with sheltering soldiers.

'What?' he yelled back. I thought better of it. Who would we signal? The artillery would just shell us and there was only the rest of the regiment in our trenches but no one would see it. I spotted a shell hole just five feet away. If I crawled, I might make it, I thought. If I crouched, there wouldn't be much chance, but I might make it. If I walked upright, I'd never make it. Here goes nothing I thought. Then I saw some of the German soldiers wearing gas tanks. Then I understood. Flamethrowers. They could burn you alive if you were within range. I saw them spray the ignited petrol making a shield of heat and flames.

'Oh, come on,' one soldier cursed. 'How do we get 'em now Cap'n. We're gonnered now.' I took the flames as another thing. A curtain. They couldn't see what we were doing now and the heat was so unbearably hot, you couldn't see anything unless you went close enough. I crept towards the shell hole and crouched down.

'Cap'n,' the soldier who had complained said. 'Come on. I thought you were the boss. You ain't doing nothing. 'E's doing all the thinking.'

I couldn't see a thing through the thick sheet of flames, but that didn't matter. We were piling up sandbags for cover. Some were even hiding behind boxes. Captain Miltain started to organise us into lines of fifteen. The plan was to always have an attack and cover squad. I was in the first squad, along with Harley and Darren. The rest I didn't know. We would wait until the fire separating us was low enough to jump over. Then the attack squad would throw one grenade each and run to find cover quickly. Every thirty seconds a new wave would arrive.

Eventually, the flames died down. As soon as the order was given we threw our grenades. 'Charge,' Captain Miltain shouted. I prayed inside my head, knowing that any second a bullet would arrive with my name on it. The German soldiers were shocked and took a moment to react, giving me enough time to take cover. They fired their first bullets just as I reached a small hole.

The second wave started, covered by the third wave. And so on and on, until the Germans found out our plan and started to destroy it. There were about two hundred men sheltering from the firing, fifty wounded or dead. A wounded German soldier managed to reach the shelter I was hiding in. He looked helpless, reaching our to me with his hand.

'What's it look like on your side?' I asked him. 'Where are they positioned?' The soldier took deep breaths. But he didn't say anything. I saw a bullet wound in his chest.

'They are devils,' he managed to say in rusty English. 'I always supported you. Kaiser Wilhelm is what you call a bastard. I am happy you have made this misery end. Danke.' Then a shot rang out and he slumped over dead. I was perplexed by what he'd said and what had happened. I don't know why but I felt tears rolling down from my eyes. I felt a shadow over me. 'Why did you kill him?' I asked. The soldier shrugged. He opened his mouth. 'Why the hell did you not kill him? You'd be dead if it weren't for me.' I stood up.

'Yeah, well some Germans aren't as evil as you think they are.' I lifted the German up and carried him in a way I had learnt at training. His chin on my chest and his legs over my shoulder. I knew he was dead. But I wanted to bury him. I carried him all the way to a shell hole and left him there. I'll be back, I promised myself. I'll be back.

'Don't let them get us,' Captain Miltain bellowed. But we were running out of ammunition, so it was hard to retrieve bullets from fallen soldiers. The fire was starting to deafen my ears. 'Hide!' Captain Miltain commanded. 'In thirty seconds we'll charge.' I nodded, glad that this was the only chance we'd get to survive.

'Now!' Captain Miltain bellowed. We surged forward, upon the German soldiers who were simply overwhelmed but put up a valiant fight. There was no time to stop. It was now or never. The remaining Germans surrendered or ran off. Many cheered, but everyone knew that they had simply retreated to another line of trenches. Signalers signaled that we had won. And we were on stand-to in trenches in case they decided to come back with help.

'Where do you get a haircut?' I asked Lenny, for he usually knew these things and he had had one only last month. 'There's this bloke,' Lenny replied. 'Dunno what he's called… Private Tend or something. 'E's actually pretty decent. Got this hair spray that keeps the rats away. I bought it for five bob. It was worth it. No rats for about two weeks. I ran out 'cos I sprayed it wherever I sat down. Even sprayed my clothes with it.' I did remember Lenny smelling weird.

I heard the marching of the rest of the regiment approaching. 'We're splitting up,' Lenny said. I looked at him. 'What?' I asked. 'How do you know this? I thought we were going to the Somme. Why would we split up? I thought our battalions was gonna meet up with the rest of the reg and we'd meet up at the Somme together.' Lenny shook his head. How did he find these things out, I asked myself?

'They say we're gonna get there faster if we split up 'cos if there's less of us we'll cover more ground. It may be true. But if we get attacked by Fritz and they're in greater numbers we don't stand a chance. They're the blimmin' German Empire for Lord's sake. I'm pretty sure Harley told me that they beat the Russians and France and all that. Load of codswallop, I think this Somme offensive is. Say we're gonna do this and then we'll be all the way back home to Blighty in no time.' I nodded vaguely.

By five o'clock some troops had left for the Somme whilst our battalion made camp. I started to dig the German soldier's grave when the sun was beginning to set. When I lowered him into the hole, I felt something in his breast pocket. I pulled it out. It was a letter from his mother. I uncrumpled it and smoothed it out. I went to a soldier who knew a little German and asked him to read it out for me:

My dear Walter,

I hope you do survive that push that you were rumoured to do. Only last Friday a couple of soldiers came to the farm and demanded food. You are so right about not trusting them. Everyone expects us to treat the soldiers on leave like saints, but they're not all good folks. There is some happy news of late though. Lu-Lu has given birth to the most adorable snow white puppies I have ever laid eyes on. Peter wishes he could come with you to help and be with you, but your Father will not hear of it. Although Peter is fifteen he is always asking about it. We are having to work constantly because the soldiers need food and lots of it. I have to sometimes help make uniforms and your Father works on machinery when they "pop" by. Very soon they say the war will be over and then you can come home. I shall see you soon.

Your mother

Most soldiers were now leaning against walls chatting with cigarettes in their mouths. Happy. I was the opposite. Walter had had a brother. He had had a home. And now no one would ever see him again. I tucked the letter into his breast pocket and laid him down to rest. 'I'm sorry,' I murmured.

I joined Fred who was drinking beer and smoking. 'What's wrong?' he asked. 'I saw you making a grave for someone. Who was it?' I didn't reply for a while.

'A friend who was an enemy. A German.' Fred looked surprised. But he thought for a bit and understood.

'I know,' he said. 'It's unfair, innit. Some of our enemies are good. But some are bad. That's the hard bit. How do you know he was good? If he was the one I saw trying to stab you with a bayonet then he's a real Fritz for sure.' I thought about it for a moment. He had tried to stab me to make it look real.

'He wouldn't've stabbed me,' I told him.

'How do y'know?' Fred asked. 'Unless he was putting on a show then of course he would've stabbed you.'

'No, he wouldn't,' I said, 'because he was putting on a show. He hated Wilhelm or whatever his name is. He wanted to die. He hated fighting for a country that he didn't want to fight for. Now you know. You can laugh at how unpatriotic you think he was.' The truth was whether he was good or bad, he was just another guy lost in this bloody and senseless war. I stormed off to a dugout where I stayed for the rest of the night.

How Is This Home?

I trudged down the lane with a sack slung over my back chatting to Fred and Harley. I looked at the streets and the shops. Only retired men sat in the pub and women in the streets. I couldn't believe it: how was this Penge? How was this home?

'Just one more street to go,' Fred sang cheerfully.

'Can't wait to see Mango,' Harley said.

'Can't wait to see my bed,' I laughed.

And then we turned onto our road and I could see our wooden gate, and sitting on a chair, waiting outside, was Mother. She turned and I could see tears in her eyes as she beamed at us.

I ran down the road and flung myself into Mother's arms.

After she had finished hugging us Mother led us into the house where a hot bowl of steaming chicken soup was waiting for us. I picked up my spoon right away and gulped down my first spoonful, burning my throat in the attempt as I had forgotten quite how hot soup can be.

Whilst we ate Mother peppered us with questions before coming to Father.

'So,' she said. 'How is the old man?'

'Fine,' Harley replied. 'Bit busy planning stuff. Day and night nowadays. You can see the lamp in his dugout at midnight sometimes, if you park yourself in front of his dugout. They're planning something big.'

Mother took this in and went to put on the kettle.

I scraped the last of my soup out of my bowl and did a big 'ahhh' of satisfaction.

'Enjoyed that, did you?' Mother asked, smiling.

'Loved it,' I replied.

'Got a surprise for you,' she said.

'What is it?'

'Come and see.'

I got up and followed her. Harley imitated me while Fred moved on to Harley's bowl.

In the sitting room I saw a great big lump leap at my head and a cacophony of howls and yelps and all sorts of happy noises.

I also heard a sound of squeaking. I turned and saw a tiny puppy about as thick as my arm and shorter than it too.

'You bought it?' I asked in astonishment.

'No,' Mother beamed. 'Found it by the stream you like. Couldn't find the rest of its litter.'

'What breed is it?' Harley asked.

'A mongrel,' Mother told us. 'About two months old.'

'What's it called,' I asked.

'I don't know,' Mother said. 'I only found it about a week ago.'

'Is it a boy or a girl?' I asked.

'Girl,' Mother told me.

'Then we should call it Mara,' I said firmly.

'Mara it is then,' Mother smiled.

And instantly Mara became one of the family. I would like to cuddle next to her at night, lying on my heart whilst Mango squashed my legs in an attempt to get comfortable.

Mango loved Mara and Mara loved Mango. I would walk them both towards the stream where Mango would splash about but Mara would always hover on the banks.

Fred would lift them onto his lap when we were relaxing in the sitting room.

Life seemed normal. Although it wasn't.

The army had given us a week's leave and sent us home, but during that time we had to do a parade to 'up' people's spirits and so that lads could see how 'great' we were and they would want to join up.

They had started sending letters to lads who hadn't registered warning them that they were to come to the recruitment office and warning them they'd be in trouble if they didn't.

Personally, I thought it was blackmail. But apparently the government thought it necessary.

Sometimes, I'd run into Lenny or Darren who cooed over Mara. I received a letter from the army saying that we were to do the parade the next morning. I didn't get why we were doing it. Weren't we supposed to be on leave? It's not like we only needed a day or two of rest.

I ran into many soldiers whilst I was on leave, and everyone would ask what was happening and what changes there had been on the front. I said that it was a stalemate and anyone who attacked lost at least a hundred men.

Many of our comrades had shell shock and when people asked questions they would cower and shudder and begin to cry. Onlookers would say they needed to go to a lunatic asylum as they obviously weren't the type who could serve King and Country.

Whenever this happened while I was there I would give them a piece of my mind, telling them that they would never believe what we'd seen. What we'd witnessed was simply unimaginable.

During my time on leave I would wander when I wasn't walking Mango and Mara, drink heavily at the pub to forget, or just find my bed and lie there. I didn't want to do anything else.

When the day for the parade came Mother bickered about our appearance with us all the way until we left.

Hair slicked down, our uniform immaculate, we arrived at the meeting point. Crowds had begun to bunch up, knowing it was about to start. Then I saw Lieutenant Colonel Frenner and Father walk out in front of us.

'Attention,' Father called. We stood straight, backs stiff, ready to march. I saw a band start up and Lieutenant Colonel Frenner yell 'one two three four.'

We marched and as soon as we started women started screaming and throwing roses at us.

A screaming woman of about fifty hurled a rose into the air that hit me in the eye, but I did not dare move my arms from their position to rub it.

Eventually, we managed to reach a podium in the town center and we all stopped and saluted. Father took his place on the podium whilst horses jittered, women hushed, and children played around imitating our marching.

When Staff Sergeant Rough wriggled his eyebrows at a lady, I shivered in displeasure. Disgusting, I thought.

For a few minutes Father babbled on and on about how we needed women in the factories and men at the front, before he started saying that we needed men right here and now.

That got the attention of the lads in the crowd and Father started looking smug when a small, pudgy man of about thirty jumped up and shouted, 'What about my brother, eh?'

'What about your brother?' Father retorted.

'I'll tell you what, folk,' the man shouted to all of us. 'Right back at the beginning of the war he joined up. Shall I tell you how long he lasted out there?'

He waited for a second.

'Didn't even make it till Christmas. And that's when the war was supposed to be over.'

This caused a lot of disapproving muttering and Father could see that he was losing his audience.

Lieutenant Colonel Frenner spoke up: 'I'll tell you what we need. We need men. How else would we have been at peace with those Boer ruffians in South Africa? Or in any of those other countries we so rightly worked for. If we get more men, we'll have peace.'

And that worked. People cheered, the band started up again, and we were on our way.

After that parade I was exhausted. When Mother gave us a lunch of cheese and butter sandwiches, we told her about the parade. Mother pursed her lips when she heard about Father being there. 'Don't know why he won't come to see us,' she said. 'Why does he have to sleep at the barracks?'

'I dunno,' Fred answered, chomping away on an apple.

'Maybe he's planning again,' Harley pondered.

'God knows what,' I said. 'It's gonna be big. And costly.'

'Well at least I've got to see you before it,' Mother said. 'Then I'll know what you look like in your grave.'

We all chuckled but it was half-heartedly too. We didn't mean it.

On the last day of our leave I simply stayed in bed relaxing before Mother dragged me to my lukewarm porridge and told me what would happen if I didn't eat it.

After that I staggered out of the front door, pulled on my coat and shook my foot to stop Mara scratching me.

I wandered towards the recruiting office where I watched the line get ever bigger as more lads signed themselves up for death.

I pushed open the pub door and ordered a pint full of frothing beer. I took a deep sigh and drank a quarter of it in one go.

I saw all of the young men who hadn't enlisted chatting cheerfully, unlike us soldiers who limped and staggered from our war wounds and spoke darkly or sat there saying nothing.

I got drunk enough for the barman to tell me to leave; but first I swore horribly and slammed my glass down so hard it spilt over his floor.

I ended up being pushed out of the pub with him saying, 'Maybe you should be kind to the person who pays his wages to put some liquid of happiness into you drunk gamblers.'

'You think I'm a gambler, d'you,' I snarled. 'Well maybe you should show some thought to the guy who is up in France moving his backside across no man's land getting shot at every blimmin' minute, eh?'

The barman didn't seem to have an answer to this, so he slammed the door in my face and went to serve his next customer. I staggered off, spending the rest of the day in a bad mood.

'One More Push,' They Say

'One more push and they'll be back in Germany in no time. What a hiding we'll give those poor bastards. Haig says it'll be the end of the German Empire. Hey, lads?'

We were back at the front. Our new lieutenant, Lieutenant Lukey was trying to boost our confidence before we set off for the Somme. It was mid-June and they had just handed out Brodie helmets instead of caps. The Brodie helmet was a new thing that had first been handed out in April and was protecting heads from bullets.

'I said, hey lads?' Lieutenant Lukey shouted. We all agreed with a lot of muttering and dark looks. He had been taken from a training battalion and put here. 'Good, now fetch your belongings if you've left some anywhere and get ready for a long march. Report in communication trench blue in twenty minutes.' We hurried off to get our belongings.

'Do you believe what he's saying?' I asked Lenny. 'Excuse me! Excuse me.' We pushed through a crowd of lingering soldiers. Lenny shook his head.

'Haven't you heard?' he asked. 'The Germans attacked Verdun. So, it's basically just us Brits and the Germans who, in case you didn't know, are combat veterans of the highest quality. And when we regroup with our regiment, we're gonna be bamboozled by their machine guns.' 'Yeah,' I said. 'But Haig says that our artillery batteries are gonna take out their wire and strong points.'

'I know but,' Lenny explained, 'Haig wants to attack at Ypres in Belgium but instead we met at the Somme. And he wants to train our gunners and new divisions more 'cos they're inexperienced. Oh, and we're gonna be attacking in divisions as well. The more there are, the better, they say. Thirty-sixth division we're in in case you didn't know that either. So maybe you know why I'm being so negative now?' It was actually kind of impressive how much Lenny could find out. I spotted my rifle leaning against a wall.

'Well,' I said, 'There's always the chance this could go wrong. Hopefully it will.' Lenny grumbled something in reply and picked up his rifle.

'Come on. Before Lukey starts caning us like we're at school.' I nodded and went back towards communication trench blue.

The whole battalion was cramped into the trench in two columns.

'All right,' Lieutenant Colonel Frenner shouted. 'In two weeks we'll be at the Somme waiting to go into no man's land. And if you don't want to rush and then die, you should hurry up.' Five minutes later we had started marching towards the Somme.

With a bagpipe and drums we began singing. Some officers were on horseback, yelling commands to us. Gradually, we began to join the rest of our division, until the whole of the thirty second division was reunited.

'I thought we were gonna get a medal,' Lenny said, when we had made camp. 'Marching all that way. Tell you what, Alf. I'll make a deal. My 1914 star medal for a bottle of drink. Agreed?' I agreed. We traded items when we got to our tents. I took the medal in my hand and went towards Corporal Tryer's tent.

''Oo goes there?' Corporal Tryers' voice thundered. He spotted me. 'Oh,' he said. 'It's you Lance Corporal,' he sneered. 'Whatcha gonna do now, eh?' I was confused. 'Just 'cos your daddy's colonel doesn't mean you can have any right to boss me, eh. So, get lost ya filthy scumbag and don't show your face again.' I tried to reason with him. 'I said get out!' Tryer yelled. 'Get out.'

'How would you like an extra medal?' I asked. Corporal Tryer snapped out of his lousy mood. 'How much?' he demanded. 'Which medal?' I showed it to him. '1914 Star,' he muttered. I knew I had him hooked.

'Yup,' I said. 'And it's all yours for a bottle of drink. How about it?'

'Gimme,' he ordered, holding his hand out expectantly. I handed it over. I held out my hand for the bottle. Tryer didn't disappoint. He could be a lousy grouch sometimes, but he was always willing to do deals and knew a good one when he saw it. He had given me an Old Orkney which had good reviews from what I had heard. I left Tryer to his grumpiness and returned to my tent. Harley and Fred were both sitting on their beds, both with a drink in hand. I held up my bottle to them. 'Cheers,' we muttered. I drank deep into the night, until I fell into the hard mattress of my bunk.

I awoke the next morning to men having breakfast. Tents weren't as bad as trenches, so I got a better night's sleep than usual. Breakfast was lumpy bread with tea and biscuits.

'Get your beauty sleep, did you?' Fred asked. 'We're leaving in fifty minutes.'

'All right, all right,' I said. 'What's got you in a fuss?'

'Shut up,' he told me. I joined the bustling crowd around the mess tent waiting for my turn to get food.

'Alfie,' Lenny whispered.

'What,' I said. 'I don't want nothing other than food. And I mean good food.'

'You're in luck,' he grinned. 'I got some good food. Follow me.'

'What is it?' I asked. He held up a loaf of bread. 'Where the hell did you find that?' Lenny carried on walking towards the edge of the camp. 'Gimme your bayonet,' Lenny said, suddenly when we had reached the edge of the camp.

'Why?'

''Cos I said so.'

'I'm a higher rank than you.'

'I've got a loaf of nice hot bread.'

'All right. You win.'

Lenny smirked. He took my bayonet and turned it over in his hand. I spotted a small fire with a crowd huddling beside it. Lenny sliced a bit of bread off for me.

'Speer it on your bayonet,' Lenny told me. 'That's how we toast it. Oi, Fritz,' he called. I looked around and saw that a German prisoner was cutting up bread slices.

'Where'd you get all this?' I asked.

'Nicked it from Lukey,' Lenny replied casually. 'Oh, and Fritz,' he said. 'Toast them quicker. We've only got like half an hour till we leave.' I took a bite out of the buttery bread. It was delicious. After ages of lumpy bread a nice fresh loaf was heaven.

'Report for duty,' a voice boomed over the camp. Lenny groaned.

'Well,' he said. 'Best go now. Before Miltain gets up our sleeves again.'

We spent half an hour tidying this, tidying that. I was ordered to groom Captain Miltain's thoroughbred horse until it was shining. That took a while and then I had to feed it. Red, he was called. Big Red. He was a nice horse but could sometimes be a bit wild. But Captain Miltain adored him.

'Easy, boy,' I reassured Red. I eased him into his halter, feeding him oats from a bucket.

'Ah,' Captain Miltain said, entering. I straightened up and gave a stiff salute. 'At ease,' he said. I relaxed my stiff posture. 'Go on, Lance Corporal. We leave in what…' he checked his watch. 'Five minutes. Lieutenant Lukey's getting you all ready.' I left the stable, allowing Captain Miltain to stroke Red reassuringly, whispering gentle words of confidence.

In five minutes, we were marching off in two lines of formation, over hills and around lakes. Through forests and under bridges. I held my rifle by my side in case we were ambushed, Lieutenant Lukey said. After two hours I was tired and hungry. I unwrapped a piece of bread and stuffed it in my mouth. I stumbled on a small bump in the ground. All of a sudden, men started singing, and then we were all singing. God Save the King mostly. Influenced by Lieutenant Lukey who wanted us to sing professional songs that he thought were meant to be sung. I remember walking past an abandoned farmhouse. All of the animals were there, just not the humans. Horses were in their stables. Cows in their fields. Chickens in their coups. Ditches everywhere. A barn was in ashes and there were a couple of dead dogs and soldiers scattered around the farmyard. There were a few destroyed villages that we marched past. My forehead was nice and cool from the shelter of my helmet but everywhere else I was sweating.

At five o'clock we were still marching. It was after six that we made camp. Many soldiers had infected blisters and we were given medical treatment by medics. I took a swig of my Old Orkney to drown my exhaustion and fright of the upcoming weeks.

For supper they served us pea soup with lumpy bread. I could hear the ominous rumble of heavy guns. And the distant cry of men charging into no man's land. It was all so dreadful because you couldn't see where it was coming from. You didn't know whether it was a British or a French or a German who was being struck down. I finished my supper quickly and went to bed.

Ten days later we had arrived at the Somme. There were many, many trenches filled with men. Most of them from pals battalions, the favorites of the early stages of the war. I was exhausted even though it was ten in the morning. Our regiment entered the trenches in high spirits. We took our place in the trenches next to the thirty-second division. As the plan was for the artillery to bombard the Germans for five days the guns were growling at them already. They were meant to destroy their wire and bombard their dugouts, but didn't seem to be hitting the target at all. There was barely enough space to lie down without someone shouting at me. I just sheltered in a little hole in the trenches and tried to fall asleep.

Two days later I was hurrying down the trenches.

'It doesn't make sense,' Fred insisted. 'They wouldn't launch this attack if they knew it was going to fail.'

'Yeah,' I retorted, 'but the thing is. We've been planning this for months so if we just call it off everyone will think we're just pathetic. And especially now the French need us especially now cos they lost Verdun.'

'I don't care,' Fred said. 'If it won't work then Haig and Rawlinson would just call it off. It would be stupid not to.' Another shell just rocketed past us landing a few meters away from their barbed wire. 'The problem is,' I said through gritted teeth. 'Is that we're about five hundred, six hundred yards away from their front line and we've fired maybe two hundred thousand shells at them.'

'And that's the problem,' Fred said. 'We've fired about two hundred thousand shells - but none of them have reached their targets except for the odd lucky one that actually knows how to aim a heavy gun.'

'Unless you'd like to go to them and fire for them. I doubt they'd even feel the shudder. Or unless you'd like to go to Haig and tell him to call off the attack which would probably leave you at the mercy of the firing squad.' Fred thought about that for a moment before answering.

'All right you've made your point.'

'I know I have. I'm always right.'

'Are not.'

'Am.'

'Shut up.'

'Leave me alone, Private. That's an order.'

I felt a flush of success when Fred left me alone, grumbling as he went. 'All soldiers of the thirty-second division,' Brigadier Plude roared. We all stood to attention. 'Get to your trenches where we are attacking. You are not to leave, understood?' We all saluted and muttered.

Our trenches were absolutely crowded. With rats, humans and dead bodies mingling in the same trenches the smell of sweat, blood, mud and smoke was becoming unbearable. Machine gunners were at their posts in case the Germans launched an unexpected attack on us.

The day before we went up into no man's land the officers actually told us what the plan was. 'We'll be flanked on either side by the twenty ninth division and the thirty second division. Our expectations are for you to capture the Schwaben Redoubt,' Captain Ray explained. 'If everything else further along the line goes right, then we should have it secured by night fall. You are to attack at seven thirty, just before our guns stop shelling. That way the final gap will be easier. And just to help we've dug a few explosives under their strong points. The captains will be leading the way. Take cover if you get to the machine guns before the others. You're as dead as a fish out of water if you don't. Oh yeah and if you do happen to meet a nice Fritz in their trenches either knock them out or shoot the bastards to hell. Understand?' We all agreed and hurried off to do our own business. Some writing letters to their loved ones, others just sheltering from the noise in dugouts. Some nattering away a pipe or cigarette in their mouth. I poised my pencil over a piece of paper and started to write a letter to Mother.

Dear Mother,

You might know about this attack called the Somme offensive. It might've been in the papers or something. I wouldn't know. I haven't read one since I was last home on leave. We will be attacking in our divisions, and hopefully succeed in day one's objectives. They have told us that they have dug large mines under enemy strong points. They will detonate them just before we go over to attack. They have been bombarding the Germans with shells ever since we got here and I am surprised I'm not deaf. They say this will be the final push and then we will have them back in Berlin in no time. I don't believe them. Everyone's promising us low-ranked soldiers a lot of things that aren't true. I'm sure of it. I hope I will survive this and come home.

Love, Alfie

I nodded to myself and tucked into my breast pocket. I really did hope I would make it past this battle. I wanted to see this war through. I had been stupid enough to join the army within a month of the start of the war. I had been tricked. I had been tricked into thinking that we would be back home by Christmas. But I also felt a sense of resolve. I joined right at the start. I was going to leave right at the end. When every single German had either surrendered or died. I vowed that to myself.

For the rest of that night I sheltered thinking whether or not this would be the last night I would ever sleep. It wasn't safe. But nobody was firing at us. This was as good as it could get. I watched a lieutenant smoking a cigarette and reading a book. It definitely didn't matter whether you were a lieutenant or a lance corporal. All it did was give you power in the trenches. It didn't do anything to you on the battlefield. We were all just lumps of flesh and bones.

The next morning I seemed to wake all too soon.

'Mornin', Alfie,' Darren said. 'Time to get up.' I groaned. Anxiety seemed to be spreading. Many knew that they might not come home. Only the arrogant soldiers who smoked every second of the day at least looked a little less nervous.

'Best have breakfast now,' Darren said. 'Before we go up into no man's land.' Just as he said it the call for breakfast came along with its usual shout, 'If you don't want your breakfast now then enjoy having no bloody breakfast at all.'

I went to the stand and took a slice of bread and a couple of biscuits.

'Alfie,' came a shout. I turned. Lenny was standing there with his arm around Sonny. He had a bandage around his head like I had had before. I noticed that his right leg had a bandage around it too. And I noticed he had a stick leaning on a table as he leant on Lenny.

'Hiya, Alfie,' Sonny greeted. He hobbled his way towards me.

'Sonny,' I said. It had been ages since I had last seen him. 'How long have you been in hospital?' Sonny shrugged.

'A year or so. Maybe more. Maybe less. They had to do some major operations on my head. I was in a coma for a few months. I have to use a wheelchair or a crutch now. I'm no use to the army now so I'm going tomorrow. Back to Glasgow. I heard you guys are going up there in about twenty minutes.' He looked at his watch confirming it. I silently cursed. 'Well Alfie,' he said. 'This is it. I'll see you again, maybe. Good luck out there.' We shook hands, said a few parting words and I left for the trenches again.

'All right lads,' the officers were shouting. 'Do you know how far you have to move yer arses to reach those German bastards? Five hundred yards. Five hundred yards of mines, barbed wire and craters to cross. But if you look forward and keep your wits about you, you'll be just fine. Now any second those mines we planted are gonna be detonated and we'll go charging up there into no man's land. Now get to your ladders.'

July 1st 1916

I had never been as scared as I was just then. As I stumbled towards a ladder I felt a sense of dread take hold of me. All of a sudden, there were several huge explosions. The shelling from our artillery had just stopped and I knew that any second the whistle would blow. You could've heard a pin drop. Everyone was just standing petrified, waiting. And then it came.

The whistle blew and the whole of our division charged up into no man's land. Immediately, the rattle of machine guns started up, mowing down lives as if they were simply blades of grass. Instantly hundreds of men were dead. The second and third to climb up the ladders were the ones who were mostly killed barely before they had emerged from the trench.

I had felt nothing like that before and I still haven't.

You didn't listen; you heard. You didn't look; you saw. You didn't feel; you absorbed.

We walked steadily towards the Germans, our bayonets fixed, rifles loaded and ready to fire. 'Charge,' Captain Miltain yelled. As we got closer to the German line we began to run. A mine exploded and I was thrown backwards. On my stomach, I crawled into the hole the mine had created. There were several injured men lying there, some who had legs still intact but now with chunks missing. I found Fred and Lenny sheltering there. None of them were wounded except for Fred. When I first saw Fred's leg (or at least what was left of it) I felt sick. The bottom half of Fred's right leg was gone.

'Alfie!' Lenny shouted. 'You OK?' I nodded. 'Fred was next to the chap who stepped on it. Chap's dead of course. Fred got the worst of it.' I peered over the top. More men were being gunned down by the minute.

The artillery were still shelling as planned but their firing was missing and hitting us instead. 'We've gotta get out of here,' I said urgently. Lenny nodded. I looked at Fred again. I noticed that his eyes were closed.

'He's knocked out,' Lenny explained. 'From the impact.' I crawled on my stomach out of the shell hole. Lenny imitated me. 'What's the plan?' he asked me. I thought for a moment. I stood up and charged forward.

'This.'

I hadn't noticed until then how bad a job the artillery battery had done destroying the wire. The few gaps they had made were narrow and could only fit two soldiers at a time. And as I watched the soldiers attempting to squeeze past the barbed wire, they were an easy target for machine guns and were mowed down in their hundreds.

Machine gunners had begun focusing on me now. I ran towards a deep shell hole from another landmine and jumped into it, feeling an explosion behind me.

There were several dead men in it. More alive. Most of them were wounded. Lieutenant Lukey followed me into the shell hole. 'We need to wait for them to slow down their fire,' I panted. 'They'll shoot us to smithereens if we go through that wire now. There are too few gaps.'

'Wait!' Lieutenant Lukey said incredulously. 'We're nearly there for god's sake. Load your magazines. In ten we'll go out and take them back to hell. Haig's been planning this for months. We're not going to let him down. Even if Fritz shoots me up the backside I'd still attack. Three, two, one.'

I ran over a walkway and stumbled into a small shell hole filled with dirty water. A row of soldiers in front of me were scythed down with bullets skimming past me. I made it to a cart and was sent diving towards it as a rifleman fired at me. I realized a small fire was burning on it and got up to leave when a rattle of firing sent me running the only way to go: forward I managed to make it unscathed to the final line of wire.

'How's that plan going now, huh, Lieutenant?' I asked Lieutenant Lukey sarcastically. He chose to ignore me and in answer made for a gap before being shot in the arm. He cursed whilst he tried to fire at the machine gunner who had shot him.

Unfortunately, he missed him and he began blazing his machine gun around him, missing him by centimeters. I threw a grenade at him but he threw it back.

The explosion sent me flying three feet back, landing with a thump.

'Get up, Lance Corporal!' Captain Ray shouted, pulling me to my feet.

I ran forward and spotted Lieutenant Lukey who was still firing his revolver whilst writhing in pain. He threw a grenade which exploded but then an enemy grenade landed within range to kill him. Without thinking about it I rushed forward and kicked the grenade at a coil of wire.

I lifted Lieutenant Lukey over my back and carried him to a walkway where a combat medic would be sure to come.

I ran for a machine-gunning post where two guns were stationed. On my stomach I crawled the final stretch towards them and hid at the base of the sandbags. After thirty seconds of hiding there, when I heard that the two guns were reloading, I jumped up and shot thrice. I hurdled the sandbags and drove my bayonet into the leg of the astounded assistant. I knew he hadn't been firing one of the guns, because he was covered in ammunition.

'How did they know?' I asked the German, threatening him with my bayonet. 'How did they know we were coming at this time?' He whimpered in fright and put his hands up.

'Dey listen in on telephone calls,' he said. 'The officers threaten prisoners and listen in on telephone calls. Dat is all I know.' I nodded, satisfied. I had never intended on injuring him more, but I was angry that my brother had lost his leg and wanted to find out how.

I needed to clean the German's wound, but I had no bandages. I remembered my flask of water in my rucksack and fished it out. I poured a quarter of its contents on his leg, wiped it with my cloth and handed it to him.

I left him at the post and returned to the battle. There was a mound of earth that went higher up than other machine guns and one was mounted at the top. In desperation I somehow made it there and hid there. I noticed a machine gunner who I was exposed to. I fired twice at him and crawled over there. I fired twice more at another machine gunner and his ammunition bearer and reloaded my rifle with another clip.

I spotted a soldier manning a mortar gun and I ran over to him just as his mortar ejected a rocket that flew into the air before dipping into the trench. Eventually, after about ten minutes of slaughter, we started to break through the defenses of the Schwaben Redoubt and flood the trenches. There was close combat with our artillery firing shells at us. When they were finally flushed out of their trenches we opened fire only to be waved down and having to evacuate.

We were ordered to patrol the trenches in case they were hiding. Medics were going into no man's land to carry all the casualties back into the trenches. Many, many more soldiers had been wounded or killed than I ever remembered in that whole war.

Fred was sent to the nearest hospital to have a major operation on his legs. I escorted soldiers to the field hospital set up just away from the trenches. I could see that every doctor or nurse or medic was at pains to see all the wounded. There were sights one could never forget. Sights that can haunt your nightmares. It was only at ten or so that we were sure that we could stop looking for the Germans.

For three hours I searched for Lenny, Darren and Harley. I was beginning to fear the worst when I heard the dreaded cry go up.

'Gas, gas, gas!'

There was immediate panic. Many soldiers wounded in the trenches needed help putting on a gas mask. 'Help!' a soldier cried. I ran over to him and reached into his rucksack for his mask. Gas was filling up the trenches only thirty meters away. I pulled his over his face, then rifled through my rucksack for mine.

Five yards away.

I got my mask on, one second too late. I could feel my breathing slowing down, my throat felt like starch and my eyes were filling up. I collapsed on the floor and felt my face exposed to air.

A couple of minutes later I woke up. I swore as much as I could, followed by a fit of coughing. 'Good to see you're awake, Alf.' I looked up. Harley, Lenny and Darren were standing over me. 'How're you feeling?' Lenny asked.

I grinned sarcastically before vomiting all over my uniform. 'Never better, Mr Lucky.'

'Shut up,' Lenny retorted. I called Lenny that because he had never once been sent to the hospital and had never even come close to getting injured. 'How many of us did the gas kill?' I asked. 'Surprisingly,' Darren said, 'only about fifty. But we lost so many in battle. What, it was like one thousand or something. Damn that Haig.' I joined in cursing him then remembered the German lying wounded at the machine-gunning post.

'All right, lads,' Captain Miltain yelled. 'Today's not done yet.'

A shell exploded to my right. 'You see that fort up there?' He pointed up the hill. 'Well, that's the Schwaben Redoubt and that's our objective for today. I'll give you a minute to prepare yourselves.'

So it was that we jogged up the hill under heavy fire until we managed to get close enough to fire at them. We formed a semi-circle around the front half of the fort and started suppressing it with rifle and machine gun fire. I spotted Captain Ray leading his company up a hill towards a pillbox, but saw they were suffering heavy casualties.

I knelt down and started firing at a machine gunner, until he noticed me and retaliated. I sprinted forward as I reached a line of barbed wire. I took aim at a German officer who was leading several of his men to a trench, where dozens of riflemen were firing in order at us. I lobbed a grenade into the trench but it was thrown back before it detonated. I noticed that a couple of my comrades were suppressing a position so I began to run towards them.

Mortars had begun to help against the pillboxes, which were beginning to crumble. I stumbled into a shell hole as clouds of earth filled the sky.

I sprinted towards a pillbox where a dozen Germans were clinging on to it against us. A direct hit with a mortar made it explode and we surged into the ruins.

I took aim at a machine gunner and shot him dead. Another machine gunner drew a Luger and fired it at me. It missed and I managed to hit him in the head with a piece of the pillbox.

Rallying the defenders, and with the help of machine guns, they pushed us away and set up a perimeter.

We waited for about twenty minutes after we'd been pushed out, then were suddenly getting ready to counter-attack. As Lieutenant-Colonel Frenner cried out to his battalion, I couldn't help but notice the strong defence of the Schwaben redoubt.

We charged forward yelling until we reached the first slit trenches. These were easy to clear as the occupants had mostly abandoned them by the time we reached them. The occupants of one of the slit trenches would not budge, no matter how hard we tried. It took about thirty of us before our grenades cleared it.

I saw that machine guns were being set up in a trench at the base of the redoubt which was deeper and much more fortified than the slit trenches.

As we neared it, they started the deathly rattle of machine guns, as they were simply sweeping us on to the floor.

I jumped into the trench and drove my bayonet into someone. They gasped as I pulled it back and pushed past them.

I sidestepped into a dugout and rammed a clip into my magazine. Peeking out, I saw that several others had broken into the trench but were heavily outnumbered. I re-emerged and knew that I had made a mistake - I was the only Tommy in the trench - big mistake!

I backed into the dugout but it was too late – the Germans had seen me. A hail of bullets skidded into the entrance as I prepared for the bayonet charge.

I looked out and saw a machine gun pointing at my face. I pulled it in before taking a deep breath; they had me cornered. I wouldn't be able to escape as they had a machine gun pointing at me.

To create confusion I lobbed a grenade outside and waited for the explosion. I leaped outside and engaged the machine gunners with a few rounds.

Moving on, I suppressed another German with a bayonet duel before he was joined by one of his comrades. We exchanged jabs and parries as we battled our way along the trench.

I used my rifle as a broom and 'sweeped' the mud, knocking the feet from under them.

I threw another grenade and put a bullet into both of my opponents before my comrades managed to storm the trench. The Germans headed for a trench leading into the fort and managed to block it up when they had gotten all of their men through.

Using a mortar to destroy an enemy pillbox that joined with the redoubt we flooded the ruins of it but came under swift rifle and machine gun fire.

I climbed through the wreckage and saw the tunnel leading into the fort. I fired at the backs of Germans as they scurried to safety.

I was out of sight again when I pulled out a cigarette. Putting it in the mouth of a dead comrade it looked, in the smoke, as if he were alive.

Bullets peppered his chest as I shoved him aside and fired round after round into the smoke. I joined the stampede rushing through the tunnel that was blocked by machine guns.

I downed a German soldier, then helped a Lewis gunner take control of a box of ammunition.

Smoke was causing havoc and confusion as Germans charged forward pushing us out of the pillbox.

As we evacuated the pillbox other machine guns singled us out. Passing the main trench we split up and, somehow managed to reach slit trenches and shell holes.

Hiding in a deep shell hole with Lenny, Darren, Harley and a dozen others, we slept for the rest of the night. And all that time, I couldn't help thinking about Fred, lying out there in the cold, unconscious and unsure whether or not he was going to live. Unsure whether he was even going to be found.

The Battle of the Somme

We continued suppressing the Schwaben Redoubt for about a week before the defences gave way and they moved into a village called Thiepval. We had learnt that on just that first day we suffered around sixty thousand casualties, a third of them killed.

With only limited objectives having been achieved, we had suffered all of those losses. There were no tangible gains. My battalion had suffered around two hundred casualties; the brigade about five hundred; the division about one thousand five hundred.

One hot summer's day, just a few hours after we'd gone into no man's land there was heavy shelling. We threw ourselves onto the ground and tried to find cover, but being in the middle of no man's land there was none.

'Christ,' I yelled. 'This isn't life. This is death.' I managed to find a shell hole where I hid until it stopped. I scanned up ahead for aeroplanes in case they came to look at our location. There were none.

'Those bastards,' Lenny grumbled, standing up and dusting himself. 'I swear they were aiming for me. It felt like every blimmin' shell those Fritz's fired at us was aimed at or around me.' I could see there was a change in Lenny. He was more mature, not as jokey and relaxed as he used to be. Older, more serious. But still Lenny. 'Anyway,' he said. 'We're gonna blow them to smithereens soon. All the way to Berlin. I'd do it all myself if I wanted to except that would be a suicide mission.'

We felt disgruntled on the march to where we would rest from then on, wary of the shells, of the gunshots, weary of all the danger we were in. Navigators with maps and telescopes; signalers with light signal equipment or flags. Medics with their first aid kits and helmets gleaming on their heads. Soldiers stumbling along, drunk with fatigue, using every muscle in our body once too many times with each movement.

When we got to a little town just a mile from the river Somme in blazing hot August weather we were lavished with kindness and gratefulness; grateful that we were freeing them from dreaded Germans. I lounged in a half-destroyed cafe, drinking tankards of beer, laughing and singing. I toasted Sonny and Fred. Inside my head I also toasted Mara. The Tommys were happy, as the French put it. We slipped into drunken bliss, our blood-shot eyes full of life again. I went to sleep dry, the ghost of the morning haunting me, but dry. And happy. Somehow, I was happy.

The next morning we left the town at six in the morning for we needed to get to our trenches before we started the morning attack. I was sad to see the town half destroyed and full of homeless people. I had given a bottle of wine and ten pence to one, as much as I could spare.

The trenches were full of dead Germans and rats. I slept for an hour in a dugout before waking up at the sound of shouting. 'Get up. Get up, yer lousy layabouts. We're going over in fifteen minutes so get ready. Get up.' The officers went up the line ushering everyone into their positions. I touched my heart where I kept a photograph of myself when I was six. Father was in his army uniform, buff and proud, his arm around Mother who was smiling. Fred, Harley and I were ready to go to school, caps on and grinning broadly. Mango was wagging his tail, slobbering on Harley's shoulder. It was my favorite photograph of my family.

'Get to your ladders,' a voice rang out. 'Ready.' The whistle blew. Half a dozen whistles blew and we trampled each other to get up the ladders. The first to go up were mostly the ones who made it furthest. Everyone jostled to get up and find cover as quickly as possible.

I jogged through a puddle of mud and over a walkway. I fired once at a German soldier who was firing from a rifle but missed. 'Hurry up, lads,' an officer shouted. 'Forward is the quickest way to home unless your home is with the firing squad.'

I started picking up pace until I was running. I spotted a flaw in their defence. You could jump the barbed wire. It was stupid. But if I pulled it off it could work.

'Lance Corporal,' Captain Miltain yelled. 'What are you doing.'

'Being the hero, sir,' I yelled back in reply. Without thinking I ran as fast as I could. I leaped over the wire, snagging my left leg on it. I landed badly on my right leg and collapsed exhausted. 'Alfie,' Harley called. He rushed up to me. 'Oh God,' he panted. 'Oh God.' I hadn't noticed that my left leg had a deep cut on it. He started to drag me back towards our own lines. 'Don't you worr...'

Three bullets propelled him backwards. One in the belly, one right in the heart, the last right in the neck. I screamed as I felt his pulse. Nothing. Bullets began kicking up mud around me and I looked into the eyes of my brother's killer. I encased Harley's lifeless body with my own, wincing as every fleck of mud hit me. Risking it, I reached for my rifle and brang it up to my right eye. I felt the stock jolt back into my shoulder, but it was worth it, seeing the German collapse. Gritting my teeth, I lugged Harley's limp corpse towards a small ridge, praying a stray bullet wouldn't find its mark.

I decided this would be my place in the battle. And I wouldn't leave it no matter what. As if to test my obedience to this pledge, a shell exploded, just out of range, showering me with dust, dirt and debris.

For a few hours, there was deadlock - none of us could decide the victor. Occasionally, a squad would make it into the trenches, gaining a few yards, but backup never came, so they would always be wiped out within minutes.

At one point a Lewis gunner was next to me, blazing his arsenal of ammo. But he was shot after ten minutes, turning a deathly pale as his blood soaked into the mud. There was nothing I could do.

When my rifle ammunition had run out, I used the dead Lewis gunner's machine gun. And the bower I felt as it sort of crackled and spat its bullets.

Eventually, I succumbed to my wounds, passing out as the battle raged on. When I was awakening in my groggy form, I saw a pair of men trudge over to me. But it was too much effort to keep my eyes open. As they neared I heard one recognise me. 'Ain't that old Tuck. With the dad oo's a Colonel?'

'Reckon you're right mate,' the other one said. 'Who's this guy?' He must've picked up Harley, because I heard them inhale sharply before muttering. Then we were stretchered away.

A Goddamn War

Two months later it was October. The rain was beating down on me where I lay curled up on the edge of a dugout. I had been sent to hospital for a few weeks when I had been buried alive but been sent back before the end of August. We were getting cold coughs from the rain and we were losing spirit rapidly. Our division was losing confidence that this plan would work, but still we soldiered on fighting our battles as hard as we could. That is how we never lost. We never gave up. I had just written to Mother, but I was telling too many lies. I had written that it was cold and wet and miserable but that other than that it wasn't so bad. I scribbled it all out and wrote a new one on the other side.

Dear Mother,

I hope you are having an enjoyable time in Blighty. That is what us British call home now. Blighty. So I will call it that. You may have seen in the lists of wounded or from a letter that Fred has unfortunately lost his legs on the first day of this so called 'Somme Offensive'. And in August Harley nearly died from machine gun wounds. He is in hospital about ten miles from the front. They will send him home when he has had his final operation on his lungs. I myself am fine. It is raining now and we have to march all day long even if it is raining cats and dogs. They will send Fred and Harley home soon. I am sure of it. I will come home soon, safe and alive.

Your Alfie

I stared at the letter with all those grim thoughts on it. It was very grim but it was the truth. I didn't want Mother thinking I was having a fine time. It may be hard to even imagine the sights I saw on the battlefield. But she needed to know at least some of it. She had written at least once a week to me. Unlike Father she had welcomed me home when I had had time on leave. Father had written once and I hadn't seen him for months. He had been hiding out in the dugouts and where was he now? With Haig and all the other cowardly officers waiting for us to do all the hard work whilst they smoked their pipes, polished their medals and moved figures around a map as if they were playing chess.

'Get to your ladders,' a voice shouted. 'Everyone get to your ladders.' I stood up. This was unusual. We had done an attack at eight which had been highly successful. I sighed and exited the dugout cowering from the never-ending downpour.

'Cap'n?' I asked Captain Miltain. 'Can't we just do it later. My cape's already soaked, as are my rucksack and uniform.' But Captain Miltaon shook his head.

'We've got orders from HQ that we are to attack at once. Now get to your ladder.' He steered me to a ladder before climbing up the one next to it. He took out a whistle and put it in his mouth. The same was repeated all down the line where Captains were getting ready for the dash across no man's land. He blew his whistle and jumped out of the trench followed immediately by us.

We walked steadily towards Fritz, our rifles at chest level, not faltering until we were fired at with machine guns. We picked up speed jogging towards our fate. I lifted my rifle to my eye and pulled the trigger. There were dying trees on flame everywhere. Suddenly, a shell erupted beside me. Shells were erupting everywhere. Getting concerned now I wanted to know why they had sent us into no man's land at six thirty in the afternoon. I heard the crump of a shell colliding with the sludge and I was thrown backwards, onto my back, my rifle flying out of my hands. The machine guns opened up on me and I was forced to crawl to a crater which was a few meters away. There was no one in it but a few rats and a rotting corpse. I looked out of the top and saw a dreadful sight. The thirty fourth division (or at least what was left of it) were either hanging on barbed wire or attempting to break through it.

Feeling that I needed to help I charged forward before I realised I had no rifle. It was somewhere in a ditch or a shell hole but the firing system would be jammed for sure. Racing forward, I searched for a rifle.

'Run for your lives,' Captain Ray shouted. 'Never cease. Fire.' A whizzbang went off just over my head and I was forced to throw myself onto the ground. Lenny was lying at the edge of a shell hole waiting for an opportunity to escape. Lenny made up his mind and scrambled out of it. There was immediately a burst of machine gun fire and he returned to the shell hole panting. Yellow flashes of light fired past me missing me by inches. 'Lenny,' I yelled, jumping into the crater hotly pursued by rifle fire. Lenny looked at me. I followed him as he went up, up the crumbling debris and tons of mud. I fired at a German once but missed by a foot.

We broke through the wire in twos and threes, firing at machine gunners. Eventually, they retreated and we milled around the line of trenches on stand to smoking and nattering.

'Hey,' I went up to Lenny. 'Cigarette?' He nodded but I could tell that he was being vague. There was a letter in his hand. I knew he didn't get any letters because his father was always drunk and they were always shouting at each other. The handwriting was in loopy writing that I had never dreamed of writing in. 'Maybe you should read this,' Lenny said, biting his lip. He handed it over. I ripped open the envelope and read the letter.

Alfred Tuck

On the third of September your brother, Harley Tuck, died. We believe you were with him when he died. This is why you are the first to take note of this. God bless.

I looked up at Lenny, my eyes wet with tears. 'The date says this was posted on the eleventh,' I said, croakily. 'And it's the twentieth now.' I showed Lenny the date on the letter. 4.9.1916. Lenny looked guiltily at this information. 'How long have you had this?' I asked Lenny.

'Couple of days or so,' he replied.

'Why would you do that?' I asked him, fuming.

'Ok,' Lenny retorted. 'How else would you like me to do it? Oh Alfie. I'm so sorry that your brother snuffed it.'

'If you don't bugger off, Private,' I growled, 'I will personally send you on a solo patrol into no man's land.'

'Like hell,' Lenny answered back angrily. 'The only thing you even care about is power now. Do you even care about your mates?'

'You fiend,' I exclaimed. 'Of course I care about you all. My brother died a week ago and it's because of this goddamn war.'

'Oh well you don't show it that well,' Lenny snarled back. 'Alfred Tuck, son of Colonel Tuck, the big Lance Corporal. Well, I'll tell you what you are. You're a bloody coward.'

He stormed off. I stood speechless for a moment before sitting down and crying.

Flanders Fields

It was February, just after the battle of the Somme when we heard the news. We were going to Belgium where we were to join the battles that were occurring in Ypres. Morale was high and try as they might, the officers couldn't cheer us up. We simply marched along the roads and fields, all of us lost in our own thoughts. Too morose or glum, too defeated. Many simply gave up hope and deserted. We were starting to believe that we might actually lose the war. The Eastern front was doing no better than the Western front. The Russians had a revolution going on and were having riots in the streets. They were beginning to withdraw further and further. And still the Americans had not joined the war. It was seemingly hopeless.

Marching along a field I started to feel exhausted. We were marching along to Flanders Fields near Ypres where we would be awaiting orders. But it was rumoured that hundreds of thousands of men from a huge variety of countries had either been killed, wounded or missing in action on that battlefield. I was not looking forward to Belgium.

I took out a piece of wrapped bread and ate it in crumbling pieces. I could hear the pounding of the guns in France and Belgium and prayed that one of them would not hit me. I was the last Tuck standing. Fred had been discharged of the military and was sent back home to Blighty in March. Meanwhile Harley was lying in a grave, without even a coffin, just a cross and an inscription of his name, date of birth and death and his last words. Father was also in hospital with a grenade shrapnel halfway up his leg. I hadn't heard from Mother for a while now. She had stopped writing letters and if she did it was only a telegram.

I felt truly alone without Lenny and Darren who was going back and forth between the two of us.

'We're nearly there,' Lieutenant Netford announced. 'Just another ten miles and we'll be there.' Nobody paid him any attention. We had split up into one brigade each until we received orders from High command. This way we would be able to cover more ground. It was only ten in the morning so we would get there by nightfall. There hadn't been any battles since the battle of the Somme. But I didn't care. I was too haunted by it. I was sure I wouldn't make it past whatever Headquarters was planning.

'For he's a jolly good fella,' a soldier behind me hummed. 'For he's a jolly good fella, for he's a jolly good fella,' he paused. 'Which nobody can deny.'

'Nice tune you got there mate,' I told him.

'Thanks,' he said. 'Learnt it back home. When I was five. Favorite song ever.'

Before you knew it we were all chanting along. We all had different tunes but it lifted our spirits nonetheless. After all, nothing can be perfect when you have three thousand men. Ambling along on his horse, Captain Miltain waved his finger in the air as if he were conducting us.

All of a sudden, we began to hear the shrieks and whistles and crumps of the front line. We were there. We came across soldiers, limping along, wishing us luck. Then I spotted the field hospital where all the recent injuries were being tended to. There were horrible sights that no one can erase from their memory. Everyone seemed to be busy, cleaning their rifle, returning to the line, cleaning wounds. We had not been prepared for this. This was where I learnt how awful trench warfare really was.

The trenches were dug roughly and there were no wooden planks to hold the walls up. It was simply the dirt with no sandbags at the top. Men were lying on the slants, their rifles poking out a bit. 'Settle in, lads,' the officers said, leading their men to various parts of the line. 'We're gonna be here for quite a while and this ain't exactly the friendliest place on the Western front.' I unwrapped a letter

I had received the day before from Mother and started to read it.

Dearest Alfie,

I have heard that you are going to Belgium soon which I hope is not true. There are lots of the bloodiest fighting going on in that country. The reason I have not written to you recently is because I have not had much time. We women are the only ones who are in Penge nowadays so we are having to help out in the men's old jobs. I am sewing pouches and uniforms for soldiers and sometimes go to the local factory to help with cooking or packaging. So many of the young men who have gone off won't be coming back because they have been killed. We did have the good news that Herbert White was captured by the Ottoman Empire on the beaches of Gallipoli whilst leading an assault force on them. At least he is alive. But not many others are. All the other mothers and sisters or wives cannot bear opening letters in case it bears the news they dread. The world is almost a different place. Zeppelins and U-boats are turning it morose and starving it into surrender. I fear their plan is working and if the Americans or somebody else does not join this war, I fear we will lose. I got the news that our dear Harley shall not be coming home. They say he died of chest wounds in France. I do not wish to talk about it as I still cannot believe that such a kind, loving boy can have died. But of course it must be worse for you as you were there. I shall not see your father again as he has broken a promise. And instead he gets a ticket home. I hold him he is responsible and I cannot even imagine forgiving him. Harley was such a loving boy and I still cannot imagine him in a soldier's uniform fighting for "King and Country". I am so sad you are not with me, Mango and Mara.

Your Mother

I wiped a few tears from my eye and thought if the war was so bad that women were having to do all the jobs then it was much worse than I had anticipated.

All of a sudden a huge whizzbang landed in one of our trenches. 'Take cover,' an officer yelled. 'Get to a dugout.' We all rushed to dugouts cowering from the noises. Shells were falling just outside the entrance of the dugout I was hiding in. Then I heard the drone and chatter of a machine I had only ever glimpsed from a distance before: a fighter plane. It sounded like there was a dogfight but nonetheless men were being strafed in the trenches. For hours they lobbed shells and whizzbangs over our heads.

When it did stop, I stood waiting for the Germans to attack like they mostly did after an aerial assault. True enough, after five minutes we heard them coming. Waves of men were gunned down, others simply ran until they were halted by the wire. The ones who survived either deserted or were captured. It was over very quickly by which time I had barely fired two shots. To be honest, I barely realised what had happened. Each battle was becoming something of a blur to me. And that was only the first of many more in the following weeks. In Flanders it was simply death, or survival.

'Hey, Alfie,' Darren said, walking, up to me. 'You OK? You look like you've just seen a ghost.'

'Yeah,' I replied. 'I'm fine. What's wrong?'

'Lenny's wrong,' he said. 'Not me. And so are you.'

'I'm doing just fine,' I answered shortly. 'And I don't want to talk about Lenny.'

'You need him,' Darren told me. 'And he needs you. You need each other. Most of all because of this war.'

'I don't need that guy at all and what's more I never needed him.'

'What about that time when you were getting beaten up by Tom?'

'What about it?'

'He's the one who got the blimmin' Sergeant in the first place.'

'Says who?'

'Says me. And I would know. You were fighting like a puppy. If Lenny hadn't helped, you'd have been finished.'

'No I wouldn't.'

'You still need each other,' Darren insisted. 'Don't go to your grave without forgiving each other.'

'Well, that's a little bit of a problem, Darren,' I said, 'because my brother's in his grave and it's Lenny's fault that he gave the letter a week late.'

'What letter?' Darren asked, confused.

'The goddamn letter that they gave to him confirming Harley's death. One week later he brought it. He had been hiding it. The bugger hid it. And I'm not going to be as big a bugger as he is.'

'I know you're angry but it's not in your blood to not forgive. You want to know why?'

'Yes please,' I asked sarcastically. 'Tell me why it's not in my blood to give him a piece of my mind.'

'Because you're too much of a hero,' Darren explained. 'You've got the Albert medal for saving one life even though you've saved loads more than one.'

'That's just being me,' I told him. 'How's it in my blood?'

'Because your father's got the Albert medal and god knows how many others.'

'So?'

'Harley had the Distinguished Conduct medal for saving your life.'

'He's my brother.'

'And he got the best medal in the British Army second only to the Victoria Cross.'

'That's great, geek.'

'And at the rate you're going you're gonna swipe the Victoria Cross.'

'I don't care about medals. I care about getting out of this godforsaken war. The Western front is a failure and we're now in Belgium where we're going to get ordered to our next onslaught. This is a disaster.'

I stormed off leaving Darren standing there.

Within a few months we had received orders for where we would be advancing to. We were going to be part of the third battle of Ypres near the tiny Belgian town of Passchendaele. The French and Belgian troops would be by our side. We would leave in a week. I was put in charge of setting up new machine guns that day and that was what I did all day. I heaved a machine gun to one post then to the next. I was exhausted by noon. I piled on more sandbags to the top of the trenches and filed into the lunch line for some bully beef. A new company was marching about the tents towards the line. All I knew was that they were in for a shock.

The next day we were put into the reserve trench where we could rest for a few days. It was neither comfortable nor relaxing for we had to listen to the drone and hum of the planes, rumble of bombs and chatter of machine gun fire. I had heard many stories of being attacked by cavalry but hoped it would never happen. They would trample over the tents and stab everyone with their swords. It was impossible to stop them.

We were lying on the muck waiting for the signal for us to go up into no man's land. I looked up and saw a raven take flight.

The next morning we were being rallied into our positions for a morning attack. 'One pace up,' the Major commanded. We slithered further up the trench wall which allowed us to since it was on a slant. 'Ready…' And finally the whistle blew.

We stampeded out of the trenches trampling through puddles and surging over the walkways. I took aim when I had reached a line of wire but didn't fire. I followed a sergeant around the wire but threw myself into a shell hole just as the sergeant was gunned down.

I jumped out of it and climbed over a tank that was half stuck in the mud. A mortar missed my helmet by one foot and threw my bum onto the mud on the other side of the tank. Getting up again I fired a shot at the trench.

Somehow, I managed to weave my way through the wire. I passed a dead Belgian soldier who was hiding behind a fake horse, a sniper rifle in his hands. We used fake horses to fire from in safety and to spy on German activity from close range.

Bent double I fired five shots at a machine gunning post isolated from the trenches. I loaded my magazine so that it was full and charged towards it. There was no one there but I still did not feel certain. Five more soldiers followed me in.

'Jesus,' one gasped. 'How much ammunition can you have?'

It was true. The assistant gunner was covered in coils of ammunition feeding them into the gun. I knelt by a pile of sandbags and fired at enemy gunners. Unfortunately, one spotted me.

'Get down,' I shouted just before bullets whizzed past us. But one of the soldiers crawled to the machine gun and swung it round. He loaded it and started rattling away with the gun. For thirty seconds he kept firing but he was shot in the head by an enemy sniper.

'We need to get out of here,' I cried. 'They'll pick us off here.'

'How do you intend to escape?' one soldier asked. 'They'll... like you said... pick us off.'

'I'll show you,' I said. 'Like this.'

Firing madly, I leaped out of the dugout and weaved my way through the barbed wire. But our offenses were crumbling and we were starting to retreat. I hid behind a mound of dirt and fired twice at an enemy signaler.

With an almighty cry, we gave one last charge and jumped into their trenches. But they weren't surrendering. They were brutal so we had to be brutal back. They stabbed with bayonets, shot with rifles and thumped with clubs.

After a five-minute-long free-for-all we scrambled out of the trenches running for our own line. It was no competition - with their machine guns the Germans picked us off like flies. When we did reach our trenches, we had lost about one eighth of our battalion.

The next day our rifles were inspected by none other than Staff Sergeant Rought who had recovered and was sent back to the front line. He had also been promoted from staff sergeant to sergeant first class. He looked down the end of each rifle and made his pronouncement.

'What are you doing here, Lance Corporal?' he shouted in my face.

'To fight for King and Country, Sergeant,' I replied.

'And do you know how we're gonna do that, Lance Corporal?' he asked.

'By shooting them,' I replied, realising too late that was the wrong answer.

'And will that happen if you simply act like a child, Lance Corporal?'

'No, Sergeant.'

'So, you'd better think who the devil you're talking to Lance Corporal,' he bellowed. 'Sentry duty for the next two days. Understand?'

'Yes, Sergeant.'

'Good.'

He thrust the nose of my rifle down and moved on to the next soldier.

When he had finished inspecting our rifles, he ordered us into formation and made us march in time all around the camp.

By the time it was time to polish our buttons and clean our rifles I was glad to be able to rest. I had to polish everything metal and clean the rest. I polished the buckles on my helmet thoroughly, along with all the other buckles and buttons on my uniform. My favorite way to wash my clothes was pouring hot water on them then scrubbing them for ten minutes each. I would sometimes light a fire to dry them or hang them over a washing line. This time I was drying mine on a washing line, as the sun shone. It was rare that the sun shone in Belgium.

Rubbing the bolt on my Lee-Enfield rifle I heard a shout. 'Kit inspection!' I sighed, laying down my rifle and strapping it to my back. My clothes would have to do.

Passchendaele

The next week we were marching down the streets to the village of Passchendaele. They had told us that we would be attacking the German Fourth Army and capture their U-boat ports. I had hoped we would be going back to France since I liked it there. I had very little confidence that this plan would work as the Americans were very far off and new German troops from the Eastern front were being deployed in the West.

Marching along the roads of Ypres we neared Zonnobeke, I looked at all the poppies growing on the battlefields. They were scattered around all of the fallen. All of them were growing around the deceased.

Ever since the First World War I have loved poppies. They gave all of us soldiers hope. Hope that even though we were living in a nightmare, the world may have been destroyed by soldiers, but nature was still trying to grow over the damage we had caused.

Refugees were coming up to us begging for money, some nice and some rude. One went up to Sergeant First Class Rought. This one happened to be nice.

'Please, sir,' she begged. 'I do not have enough food for my children. Please.'

'Bugger off, you homeless,' he snarled, 'before I make you.' He cocked his revolver.

The refugee bowed her head and turned to her children. A small girl about six years old and a toddler of around two. 'Is everything alright, Mama?' the little one asked.

'Yes, Tuni,' she replied. 'We will be fine.'

I looked at them and realised I should give them my water ration, a few cans of corned beef and some cold soup and bread. I hurried over to the mother who was silently crying to herself. 'Mama, look,' the girl pointed. 'A soldier is coming to us.'

The mother looked up. I held up my hands to show that I meant no harm.

'It's alright,' I reassured her. 'I've got food.' I held up the tins and water flask.

'Thank you,' the mother cried. 'Thank you. Merci. Here,' she said, offering me something in her hands. 'You may have it.' I looked at it and gasped.

It was the Victoria Cross. 'I found this on the street. You have earned it.' I took the medal but didn't pin it on my chest. I left them to huddle around a small fire heating the food up.

The medal felt cold in my pocket. I knew I couldn't keep it.

When I returned to France I would give it to someone who deserved it so much more than I did.

On July the twenty-fifth we arrived at the battlefield. The rain was battering us and the mud looked as sloppy as ever. We joined the trenches and were taken to our sector. For the next few days we were preparing for the battle.

Lying out barbed wire, setting up machine gun posts, digging ditches at our end of the battlefield; it all seemed endless.

Every day, I would return to the trenches, exhausted and cold. I'd light candles, or drink lukewarm mugs of tea. Soon even the dugouts were wet. And this was a problem for the artillery. Sometimes the telephone wires would break because of the rain and we would have to rely on other ways.

The guns would occasionally start for an hour or two but always stopped. I wish I could say the same for the rain. Even though it was July it would rain constantly, until no man's land was more like a swamp.

One day before we went over the top our artillery opened fire. Barbed wire was laid everywhere, sandbags were scattered around providing cover. And tanks were fueled up and armed. All that we needed now was for the whistle to go. Occasionally, sniper-fire started up but we usually put dummies up to figure out their positions.

Lying crippled on a bench in the trenches I started to write a letter to Fred as I had not responded to a letter I had received from him recently. He was back with Mother in Blighty and was, as he put it, 'right as rain'. He did have to get a wooden leg and was sometimes in a wheelchair, which he admitted was kind of a 'bummer'. I checked my letter for any mistakes but found nothing wrong with it. For the final time I read it out loud to myself.

Dear Fred,

How's it going? The trenches are as smelly as ever and Belgium rains too much. At least too much for my liking. And guess who's back from his "little accident"? It's only Staff Sergeant Rought except now he's been promoted to Sergeant First Class. We just call him "Sarge" or "Sergeant" though. Bit of a mouthful to say, isn't it. And how's the leg? So you've got a new one. I'm looking forward to seeing this and taking a photograph of it. And don't grumble about the wheelchair. Other lads don't have a choice. It's either you have a wheelchair or you don't walk. Sorry if I'm not helping. I don't know anything about this "not walking" thing. Lenny's ditched me and Darren's in between us. It was grand when you and Harley were here with me. I hate being lonely on the battlefield. I also hate having a shortage of beer. As I am twenty years old I am sophisticated enough to have beer. I hope you are well,

Your Lance Corporal

PS: Let Mango sleep on my bed. He must have memories or smells of me on my covers. That's an order Private!

'Alright, lads,' Sergeant First Class Rought shouted. 'Get up. Unless you want to be left to the mercy of Fritz's shells.'

I groaned and got up. The rain was still pouring. The shells were still firing. But in maybe ten or twenty minutes we'd be going into no man's land. Rubbing the sleep out of my eyes I picked up my rifle and strapped it to my back. No use using it now I thought. Captain Miltain was giving twenty men a morale speech as were the other officers. Readying myself for the battle I took out the Victoria Cross and touched the lion standing on the crown. 'God bless you, Alfie,' I whispered.

'Saying your last words are you, Tuck?' Sergeant First Class Rought sneered, strolling down the trench. 'Can't say I blame you though, can I? Those Fritzes out there are tough cookies. Some of us are sure not to make it. Still...' he paused arrogantly lighting a cigarette. 'If you keep your wits about you and look forward not backwards you could still make it.'

'I'll be fine thank you, Sergeant,' I replied. 'I'm very capable of surviving. All of us lads are.'

'Let's test that theory shall we in say,' he checked his watch, 'seven minutes.' Just at that moment all the officers started rallying their men into position. I put the Victoria Cross back into my breast pocket.

'See you, Tuck,' Sergeant First Class Rought said. 'I've gotta go rally up my men.' He left me and I felt a prod on my shoulder. It was Captain Miltain.

'Come on, Tuck,' he ordered. 'Into position.'

'Yes Captain.'

I stood back but crouched down. I spotted Lieutenant Colonel Frenner's dugout where he was planning the attack with his assistants.

His personal assistant, Lieutenant Noring came out of his dugout with the major and signaler. This was it. The major took out his watch and whistle. 'Forward.' The whole battalion heard this single word. Lieutenant Noring cocked his revolver. The same command was being given out all along the line of the attacking armies.

The shells were raining down upon us. All of a sudden, a whizzbang hit the entrance to Lieutenant Colonel Frenner's dugout.

Flames licked the dugout walls as Lieutenant Colonel Frenner retreated from them. 'Put out the damn fire.' I was stunned for a moment before I ran over to a bucket of water. I threw it onto the fire, dousing most of it out. 'Get back to your position,' Lieutenant Colonel Frenner bellowed at me.

'Yes, sir,' I said, returning to my position.

'Fix bayonets.' I fastened my bayonet to my rifle.

The rain continued to soak us but I felt it no more. The guns were more like a distant thunder.

The whistle went in the major's mouth and the flags went up in the signalers' hands. The major blew into the whistle starting the battle.

We surged forward scrambling out of the trenches and into the muck. Immediately I found myself on the ground. A soldier who had just gone up was shot in the face. I realized that if I hadn't tripped, that would have been me.

Then there was a sound. The sound of Germans coming out of their trenches. I fired at one German but missed as he was engaged in a bayonet duel. We rushed forward to meet them on the battlefield.

Crouching down behind an ambulance cart I fired a shot at a German with a trench raiding club. Crawling towards a mound of earth that provided cover and a good view, I saw one opponent coming towards me. In my haste to fire at him I was caught off guard when he was backed by a compatriot. I stood up and fired at him. Somehow, I kept on missing. I charged towards him, my bayonet raised. He disarmed me and kicked me in the chest. 'Hello, Tommy,' he snarled.

All of a sudden, he crumpled and I spotted a bullet wound in his chest. 'You big horse's arse,' a voice growled to my left. I looked but couldn't see anyone.

I spotted a tank clanking along the battlefield. It was blown up by a shell. Flames erupted. 'I need cover,' I yelled. 'Cover me.' I made my way towards the tank. There was a tiny gap through which I squeezed. I was greeted by fiery hot flames reaching towards me.

Several of the tank crew were dead but someone called out to me. 'Get out of here, lad,' he cried. 'You'll die in here.'

Ignoring him I dragged one of them out of the tank to a walkway. But the fire had intensified and I was forced to leave the rest of the tank crew.

I spotted a soldier who was fending for himself with a Lewis machine gun. Rushing over to help him I crouched down and aimed my rifle. Crowds of them were advancing towards us but with a machine gun and a decent rifle we managed to prevent them from reaching us.

Finally, after ten more minutes of fighting we managed to push them back into their trenches. I was shivering in a shell hole where we had been ordered to stay. We were told we would renew our attack shortly. We dug a small trench in which we stayed in for the rest of the day bent-double and not able to talk in anything louder than a mutter. We waited for morning, hoping we could attack then and get the breakthrough.

'Get up,' Captain Miltain hissed shaking me. 'Get up Tuck. Eat this up quick.'

He handed me a tin of soup.

I gulped it down and watched the other soldiers getting ready for the assault.

'Attention,' Captain Miltain cried.

He drew his revolver.

'Here's the plan: we sneak into their trenches, and just fire. Try and get to the dugouts.'

And with that he got on his stomach and crawled forward.

In no time we had reached their trenches and we all threw a grenade in.

The Germans were ready in an instant and those Brits who did jump into their trenches were shot before they could even make for the ladder. I threw myself down into a shell hole and looked at the view.

Germans were standing on their fire steps firing at the odd soldier and the machine guns were punching through the piles of mud some were hiding behind. I fumbled with my bayonet but pressed it on to my rifle just in time before a German staggered into my shell hole. I stared at him with his hands up but then I realized something. He was burning.

As he attempted to lob a grenade at me I kicked it away and man-handled him to the floor. He kicked back at me and ran towards his trenches. I fired once at his back but missed and I saw him fumbling for a pistol.

I took a shot at his head but it ricocheted off his German 'Stahlhelm'. He made it to his trench and fired five shots at me. I knew he would best me so I made a daring move to get closer to the trench. I made it about fifteen yards away from their trenches and could just about lob grenades at them. Suddenly, the Germans clambered out of their trenches and charged towards us. I abandoned the shell hole and ran twenty yards towards a mound of earth. I took a shot at the legs of an officer and finished him off whilst he crumpled. I crawled forward but saw the Germans had taken a dozen meters of ground and were firing from shell holes. Directly opposite me was a group of Germans in a shell hole awaiting the grenade I had lobbed into it.

The bang went off and I rushed into it, pointing my bayonet. Fortunately, the ones who were alive were too wounded to move so I called for a stretcher bearer and his assistant. They transported the wounded Germans whilst I covered. Suddenly, I heard a shell whistle and the crump as it landed nearby.

I flew into the open battlefield and crawled back into my shell hole just as two Germans entered it. I swore and grabbed a trench digging shovel and knocked one of them out. The next fired a Luger pistol at me just as I lunged at his legs. I reached for my rifle and whacked the rifle stock against his legs, making him collapse. I myself was close to collapsing and the rest of that day went by in a blur.

The next month we were trudging over a walkway amid freezing rain sometimes getting stuck in the mud. Some men were being stretchered or some being escorted. Nobody believed that there would be a breakthrough anytime soon. It seemed impossible. The Americans had just entered Europe but had not sought combat yet. Britain was the only reliable Ally left as the French were still recovering from a mutiny.

I was ordered on sentry duty for two hours whilst we waited for a cavalry charge on the Germans.

'Switch,' Sergeant First Class Rought bellowed. Gratefully I climbed down from the post where I met the next soldier for sentry duty. I was ordered to make a bridge with several others for the cavalry with scraps of wood.

'And it better be strong, mind,' the officers had reminded me. 'Cos we're gonna have several hundred horses and men trotting over us. So make it good.'

It looked decent so far. I didn't see why the horses couldn't just jump over the trenches, but I did it anyway.

When I had finished I heard a cry go up in the trenches. 'Who's a decent shot?' a voice rang out. I went to see what all the kerfuffle was about. There was a human dummy looking out of the trenches waiting to be shot at. All of a sudden, there was a hole in the dummy's left eye. I looked through the hole. There was another bang and I pulled away just in time.

'Jeeze,' one soldier said. 'That's one feisty sniper.' But when we pushed the decoy into view again there wasn't a shot. Instead, there was a rattle of machine gun fire as the dummy was obliterated.

'Duck down,' a soldier hissed. 'I said, duck down.' For some reason we all obeyed him. I lay there for a while before I was ordered to start looking out of periscopes. This and sentry duty were the most tiresome duties in the trenches as they drained your energy whilst you were simply staring into no man's land.

Hooves clattered over the deck as we cheered the cavalry on. The riders' swords glinted in the dim light. The last of the squadron clomped over the wooden bridge and started to trot. I looked out of a periscope to see them galloping into formation, shells and whizzbangs descending onto them, tossing them into the air.

Then out of nowhere some of the wounded horses started sinking in the mud. It was a horrible sight. Horses and troopers were drowning in the battlefield. Meanwhile the remaining cavalry were mowed down by machine guns until only a handful were left.

We had to wait for a few hours before it was safe to retrieve the wounded. Under heavy fire we ducked down and crawled towards the wounded. I covered some soldiers, sometimes retrieving myself. Fritz sent wave after wave of machine gun bullets at us rarely hitting us.

Suddenly, whilst I was helping to carry a man back to the trenches I felt a sinking sensation. Looking down I felt my heart sink. I was sinking in the swampy battlefield. I attempted to scramble out but it was like I was glued in. I couldn't.

'Help,' I cried. 'Help!' A soldier ran up to me and hoisted me under the armpits. That still was not enough. I threw my rifle to one side and attempted to squirm away.

'Lenny,' I recognized the voice as Darren's. 'C'm here.'

I saw Lenny take hold of one of my arms and pull. It was no use. I felt myself drowning in the pool of mud many horses and soldiers and stamped up.

'Heave,' Lenny grunted. 'Heave ho.'

I felt myself getting freer before I was hoisted out of the swamp.

'There you go mate,' Lenny patted me on the back. Suddenly, it was as if we had never not been friends. I flopped onto his shoulder and gave a hoarse sob.

'There there, Alf,' Lenny reassured. 'All's good.'

'I'm not a soldier,' I croaked. 'A lad from Penge. Not a soldier.'

'Yes you are,' Darren said. 'You're a Lance Corporal. You've got the DCM. You're as good a soldier as anyone.'

'Come on,' Lenny said. 'For Penge.'

We agreed and trudged back into the trenches where men were getting treated and horses carted to veterinary hospitals. I spent the rest of the day coughing up mud and wrestling with a thought that had been bothering me. By noon I had made up my mind. I would tell the officers what Lenny and Darren had done, how they had saved my life and that they should give them a medal. I was absolutely positive they would give them one.

I knocked on the door of Lieutenant Colonel Frenner's dugout which was occupied with him, Major Bennet, Captain Miltain, Lieutenant Netford and Sergeant First Class Rought. They looked up when I entered. 'Tuck,' they said in unison.

'What the hell are you doing here?' Sergeant First Class Rought snarled.

'I have something to say, sir.'

'What is it?' Captain Miltain asked.

'It's about Private Bowl and Eastwood, sir.'

'What about them?'

'They saved my life, sir.'

'Many people have saved many lives, Lance Corporal,' Major Bennet told me. 'You have yet to learn.'

'Yeah, but these lads did something special.'

'And what is that?'

'They used teamwork to save me. There I was drowning in that sea of mud then they came and saved me.'

'Tuck,' Major Bennet said, 'medics and doctors use teamwork to save lives every day. And they don't come asking for medals.'

'Yeah,' I reasoned, 'but if you were drowning in the mud and you were wounded then you wouldn't be able to be saved would you?'

'Yes, Lance Corporal,' Sergeant First Class Rought said sarcastically. 'We do know that.'

'And if you're wounded on the battlefield you can just get rescued by a medic.'

'So?'

'Well, if they'd just let me drown then you'd have lost one of your Lance Corporals.'

'That doesn't matter, Tuck,' Lieutenant Colonel Frenner was a bit frustrated with me now. 'Officers matter. They're the ones who plan the victories.'

'No officers don't matter, sir,' I said. 'They only matter if you need to plan something big. And you're not. You're planning slaughterhouses. Who do you reckon fights on the battlefield seeing things you can't forget? Not sitting in your dugouts looking out of flimsy periscopes.'

'Slaughterhouses, Tuck?' Major Bennet questioned incredulously. 'In case you haven't noticed we've made it to Belgium, Tuck. From England to France to Belgium. And we have halted the goddamn Germans for a pretty long time.'

'At a price of more than two million men, sir.'

'Do you know how long I have worked in the British Army, Lance Corporal? Ten years. Ten goddamn years. And you've been in it for three.'

'And for three years I've been going into no man's land seeing things you can't forget.'

'You think I haven't, Lance Corporal?' Major Bennet cried.

'Do you remember the Somme, sir?' I asked him.

'Of course I do,' he said.

'And do you know what the battlefield looked like when we'd finally pushed through?'

'Are you daft, Lance Corporal?'

'My own brother died in that slaughterhouse.'

'And it's not our bloody fault that that happened.'

'And do you know how old he was?'

'Why should I know.'

'Seventeen years old. He died when he was seventeen years old.'

'So he snuck in.'

'Of course,' I told him.

'And that means he broke the law.'

'Did you ask for all available hands or not?'

'Why yes we did.'

'Then he did not break the law. He simply bent it to help you.'

'And do you know why he died, Lance Corporal?'

'Yes I know how he died. He died trying to save me.'

'He needn't have done that.'

'But he did, sir, he did.'

'That doesn't matter. He got a Distinguished Conduct Medal. What more can you ask for?'

'Can't you just give men a chance,' I said before leaving the dugout.

And so it was that Lenny and Darren didn't get the medals that they deserved and we continued to fight the battle for weeks more. But I remember the last few days of that dreadful battle because it was one of the worst times of my life.

Some of us were sleeping in our dugouts, some of us were smoking, some were cleaning our rifles and some were drinking tea. This was disturbed by a shriek followed by a bang. I grabbed my rifle and hurried outside to see what was going on. 'Get to your dugouts!' Captain Miltain shouted as I cowered. I dived back into the dugout whilst our trench was bombarded.

I waited for the shell to come and hit me. I waited and waited but it never came. For the whole of the night it went on like this until it stopped and I heard the cry of men coming over from no man's land.

'Get out of your dugouts lads. Get out.'

We scrambled out of our dugouts and met a wave of surprise. 'It's stormtroopers,' Lenny shouted. 'German stormtroopers.' I had heard about German stormtroopers who used machine guns, grenades, rifles, pistols and flamethrowers to overrun our trenches.

'Stand your ground,' Captain Miltain ordered. We fired our machine guns and rifles at them, but they were no use. In no time at all they had broken into our trenches and had begun firing at us. I retreated further down the trench firing at them. I saw them ignite their flamethrowers, huge flames erupting from the spout.

They fixed their bayonets and started to make their way towards us. But the machine guns were the most effective. They mowed us down in our own trenches before we were able to kill one of the stormtroopers manning a machine gun. I fired at one of them. He was throwing grenades with one hand, and held a pistol in the other.

'Bayonet charge,' Captain Miltain shouted. We charged forwards glaring at the stormtroopers who increased their fire. I managed to weave past the flames of the flamethrowers and plunge my bayonet into a rifleman.

After ten minutes of close combat fighting we drove the stormtroopers out of our trenches. Immediately, the whistle went and we climbed out into no man's land. But the stormtroopers held their ground and only retreated walking backwards. As if things could not get worse the German infantry climbed out of the trenches and joined the stormtroopers.

We rushed forward firing at the stormtroopers as they gradually retreated. Men were being drowned by human hands, stabbed multiple times in the face. Once I used my rifle as a club and knocked a soldier out with it.

It was tough to dislodge the stormtroopers and with the help of the infantry they seemed unbeatable. But somehow, after heavy fighting, we managed to dislodge German troops and take hold of their trenches.

The next day we advanced into the village of Passendaele but it was more like a ruin than anything else. We had been fighting heavily in the streets. Casualties had mounted.

One morning we split up into groups of thirty under the command of Lieutenant Netford where we were to take on an enemy machine-gunning position.

We crept through the town peering down the destroyed roads. All of a sudden, we came under attack. 'Take cover!' Lieutenant Netford shouted. I hid behind a pile of timber that towered up to four feet.

'Ok lads,' Lieutenant Netford ordered. 'Ten men go left, ten right, ten straight on. Sergeants in command.' Several minutes later we set off, firing at the Germans. I ran into a shop for a few seconds before emerging.

Our squad managed to reach the machine guns and captured several Germans. We found out that there was an enemy pillbox on the other side and that we needed to eliminate it. Regrouping with the rest of the platoon we began taking out machine gunners but taking casualties ourselves.

Many of our soldiers got wounded and that made it more difficult to reach the pillbox. I threw several grenades into the pillbox and fired at the machine gunners.

'Bayonet charge,' Lieutenant Netford shouted. I ran forward until I reached the base of the pillbox. I threw a grenade through the slit where the guns pointed out and waited for the bang. Germans came rushing out until they realised we had cornered them. I fired at some of the escaping Germans and fired into the pillbox.

I didn't want to enter so I took an extended periscope from my rucksack and peered into it. I got to look into it for a second before the machine guns obliterated it; half a dozen machine guns were stationed with the barrels turned to us.

Ducking down and sidling into view I fired wildly at a machine gunner but missed. Not a second too soon I sidled back before machine guns opened up. 'Throw grenades,' Lieutenant Netford ordered. 'In the front and the back.'

I crept round the pillbox and kneeled down. I gestured for someone to get on my knee and I pushed them up. There was immediate gunfire and I saw the soldier fall out of the pillbox, a wound in his chest.

'Lift me up,' I mouthed to Lenny, who had also been chosen into the same platoon as me.

'Are you out of your mind?' Lenny asked.

'It doesn't matter,' I replied. 'Someone's gotta do it. May as well be me.'

Reluctantly, Lenny knelt down and allowed me to stand on his knee. Lifting me, I heard him mutter, 'Good luck, Alf. Don't let those Germans shoot you.'

I clung on to the gap and hoisted myself up. Unfortunately, this did not go unnoticed. A German had turned around to the noise and stuttered. I fired a moment before he had and that was all the difference it made.

The German was blasted back, killed instantly. I fumbled for a grenade before pulling the pin out and chucking it into the heart of the machine gunners just as they turned around and fired their first volley.

Somehow I managed to survive the volley of bullets, though I was hit. I was not sent to hospital as it was only my leg that was properly hurt and we were needed in as great a number as ever.

That evening we had regrouped with the rest of the battalion but now it was only about one hundred men. This was the smallest our battalion had ever been reduced to.

We were billeted in a block of houses that provided cover where we set up machine guns and sandbags. We then slept, leaning on sandbags or houses. I felt the throbbing in my leg and took a look at it. It didn't seem too bad. A few cuts and holes that had turned nasty shades of purple. I ignored them and tried to fall asleep.

I heard whizz and bang, the crump of shells colliding with their targets. 'Get up, lads,' Captain Miltain yelled. 'Get up. They're shelling us to smithereens.'

I pushed myself to my feet and took in the scene. I saw incoming Germans firing at us, shells and whizzbangs exploding everywhere.

'Attack,' Captain Miltain yelled. I saw other soldiers grabbing their rifles and running to the aid of our comrades. 'Fix bayonets… Charge.' I took cover behind a statue and fired rapidly. I threw a grenade at a squad of enemy and prayed that it would take them all out.

I heard a cry to my left and saw Anzac forces coming to our aid. The Australian and New Zealand soldiers fought ferociously and desperately.

The fighting went long into the night and we were beginning to take it in shifts to hold the line. The machine guns were the most effective so when one of our gunners was shot down I ran to his Lewis gun and began firing it.

A machine gun is one of the most feared weapons in a war as it can take out wave after wave of troops without running out of ammunition. As soon as I started the deathly machine, I regretted it. More soldiers went for me and that meant that I had no choice but to gun them down. I wanted to pull away from it but knew that I would just get fired upon, so I stayed put.

We held the enemy soldiers at bay for about half an hour before they fell back into the entrance to a museum. A broken-down tank was about fifteen meters from the entrance but the heat from the flames could've burnt us.

Taking my chances, I crouched down behind the tank. Captain Miltain rushed forward leading a dozen men, but all were scythed down except for the captain himself. I scrambled out of my position and towards a corner around the side.

When you're under fire, you can only think of one thing: forward. That is the only way to go. The adrenaline pumping through you will hopefully give you enough energy to charge forwards.

I ran round the corner and took a deep breath. I heard the machine guns but I couldn't exactly turn back. I took a quick shot at a German machine gunner but missed. I jogged forward and took cover beside some steps.

I hurled a grenade, hoping it would land in the middle of the gunners. After the blast I scurried forward and saw that not even one of them was dead. They started firing at me and I would have been hit if not for the cover fire produced by my comrades.

I crouched down and placed my rifle on top of a pile of sandbags, waiting for them to come.

And then, the full might of the German Army struck…

A section of stormtroopers were fiercely blasting us down. Trying to hold my ground I fired continuously until I was out of clips and had to lob grenades. I didn't go unnoticed for long. Their fire focused on me, behalf a German with a trench-raiding club pounced and swung at me.

I parried and ducked, but my bayonet was not good enough. I finished it by smashing my rifle stock at the soldier's hands, making him wince and drop his weapon. I managed to overcome him.

The bloodiest fighting was taking place in the houses and streets where both sides were charging at each other, bayonets sticking out the front of each soldier's gun.

Captain Miltain had handed me thirty rounds of ammunition. I followed him to a position before he ran off again. I fired at multiple Germans, each one becoming one of the hundreds that were falling. I spotted a group of injured privates huddling behind a corner; a German soldier approaching. I rushed over, just before the German shot and put a bullet into him.

'Alright, chaps,' I said to the soldiers.

''Ello, Lance Corporal,' a soldier said. 'Blimmin' party, innit?'

'I see you have a Lewis gun,' I said.

'Aye, sir.'

'Alright,' I said hurriedly. 'Fix your bayonets. C'mon lads. Quick!' But they didn't. So I did it for them. Then I put a clip into each of their rifles and told them sternly,

'When those Germans out there come over here, you shoot them! Understand?'

'Yes, sir,' they muttered, pulling themselves into position.

'Now, you need a medic. Medic? Medic?' A medic rushed over and tended to the wounded privates.

By the end of the day the battalion was reduced to sixty men, but we had pushed the Germans away from us and claimed the town of Passendaele.

Soldiers milled about, Canadian, New Zealand, and Australian and British, chatting and smoking. Stretchers had been issued and the wounded were lying on them, some wounded so badly they had passed out, others gazing into space, grimacing as the medics extracted shrapnel from their wounds or dressed an open cut.

I wandered around until I had found a medic who was free, and he tended to my leg. The field hospital was full, he said, as was the hospital behind the lines, so I was to be tended to right there, just like everyone else.

I lay there, day and night for weeks on end, my wound slowly healing. One day, about two months after I had been wounded, whilst I was lying in the grassy garden of the field hospital, watching the sun set for the last time before the year 1918 dawned, I heard voices saying my name.

When I returned to my tent I saw my doctor and a few nurses bustling about, moving medical supplies. They turned around when I hobbled in.

'Tuck,' Doctor Water said. 'How's your leg?'

'Fine, sir,' I replied. 'A bit stiff but otherwise fine.'

'Good,' Doctor Water replied. 'The front line needs you and there are only a couple dozen soldiers out there in your battalion. You will be moved back there in two days.'

And so it was that I went back to the front line, waiting with the rest of the soldiers for the next attack. Headquarters had seemed to pity us and within a week of my return we were transported to the reserve trench where we milled around sleeping in dugouts or just on the frozen mud.

Snow fell heavily that winter and we half froze to death in the trenches from the cold if one of us hadn't had the bright idea of breaking up unwanted bits from rifles and feeding them to a fire of bootlaces, wet coal and strips of wood.

Drinking also helped. Whenever we could get some time off to go to a pub in the village nearby we'd drink their good Belgian beer and wolf down egg and chips. I'd often pray in the trenches when an artillery barrage was going on. I would pray that they wouldn't attack, that they would attack the rest of the line. Not us.

Back to France and the Start of the Collapse

'So we're going back to France and that's that,' Major Bennet was giving us his 'morale speech.'

'But, sir,' one soldier piped up. 'If we go to blimmin' France again we'll get torn to pieces just like last time.'

'Just do as you're told,' Major Bennet replied. 'We're getting stationed in a quiet sector. We're to wait about two months then we'll be back in tough zone with some new recruits.'

'Fresh recruits who hardly know how to hold a rifle,' Lenny muttered under his breath.

Major Bennet overheard him.

'Yes, Eastwood,' he said. 'Fresh recruits who hardly know how to hold a rifle. But they're being taught and you'll help when they get here.'

'But we're soldiers, Maj,' a cheeky one said. 'Not teachers.'

'You'll do as you're told.'

We all grumbled. Us battle-hardy soldiers teaching new recruits how to stay awake on sentry duty and all that. Of course, the training was becoming more and more rushed as more and more troops were being wiped out by the month.

This was our third batch of new soldiers, but we were still running short on only four hundred men.

'So, Maj,' one of the soldiers asked. 'When are we going to the Bonjours? I am looking forward to it. Not as slimy the trenches over there. That's a treat right there.'

'About three weeks,' Major Bennet replied. 'But that's three weeks in which you'll make these trenches spick and span. Straight trenches; strong and sturdy, tidy dugouts and try to get as much mud and rats out as possible - we don't want the next battalion to think we're a dirty lot.'

'But we are a dirty lot, Maj,' Lenny replied cheekily. 'We're as dirty as them rats 'cept we don't eat dead bodies.'

'Yes,' Major Bennet retorted, 'and our trenches are gonna be as clean as they can be, Eastwood.'

'But look at you, sir,' Lenny joked. 'You's got your winter hat on.'

'That's 'cos it's freezing, Eastwood,' Major Bennet retorted. 'And there ain't a law that an officer can't wear a hat.'

'But we can't, sir,' Lenny protested.

'That's 'cos you haven't earned it, private. You gotta learn some discipline. Now get on with your duties, the lot of you.'

We all hurried away, hunching our backs due to the cold, and blowing on our fingers in the hope of restoring some sensation to them. I wanted to ask Mother if she could knit me some gloves or something like that.

I started mending a fallen trench. An explosion had caved in the walls and I found a few bodies in the mud. I knew at once that they were dead and carried them to the place in the trenches where soldiers were buried. When I resumed mending the trench, I saw Captain Miltain looking through a periscope into no man's land.

'What the hell,' he muttered.

'What is it, sir,' I called over.

Then I saw it. A man was hobbling over to our trenches, a white handkerchief in his left hand. His right was held to a bullet wound on his waist.

'Get someone up there,' Captain Miltain ordered. 'Tuck,' he called me over. 'Come here. We're going over the top.'

'Yes, sir,' I nodded.

'Cover fire,' Captain Miltain commanded.

Captain Miltain loaded and cocked his revolver, then he gestured for me to imitate him as he climbed up a ladder. The wounded soldier carried on hobbling towards us with a revolver in his hand. There was firing all along the line, some from us and some from the Germans. I took my greatcoat and rucksack off so that I was lighter.

Finally, the soldier met us before collapsing. I ducked down and hoisted him up. Captain Miltain covered me by standing in front of me and firing. I had put my arm under his and laid it behind his neck then Captain Miltain did the same.

The soldier had regained a little consciousness and had started to limp forward to help. Luckily, none of the firing had hit us until we got about halfway back from where the man had fallen.

He cried out in pain and collapsed. I ducked down to see what was wrong. He had been shot in the arm, almost certainly breaking it. But that was not the end of it. As we hoisted him up again Captain Miltain was shot in the leg. He toppled over, clutching his leg.

'Get the wounded back into the trenches,' Captain Miltain gasped. 'They'll come for me later.'

I carried the soldier back into our trenches before returning to Captain Miltain and helping him back into our trenches before he was stretchered away.

That night I didn't sleep well. I kept thinking about the soldier who had been escaping from the Germans. But why?

We were on our way to France, marching and marching, taking the train sometimes. But this time we had brought a new type of ferocity. The enemy had practically wiped out our entire battalion! But we'd been in this war from the start. We were going to see this through to the last man.

When we were on the train we wouldn't drink beer and cider like we'd used to; we sat in the carriages looking out of the window, or just dozing, as we rarely got the chance to in the trenches. Some of us would just gaze into space, too lost in our misery.

But when we were on foot there was more heart put into it. We would still trudge along, muttering about the blisters on our feet, but we'd look up not down.

We were going to France, we thought, where we'd be with the Americans and the French. In Belgium we'd been isolated. It had only been us Brits and a few Belgian troops, whereas in France I was sure there would be more help, more support. Then again, it was all still the same horror; the same war; the same world.

One day when we were on the border of Belgium and France I spotted another field of poppies. As we marched through them I stooped down and plucked a few. I weaved the stem through my uniform until it stuck on my chest. I looked down upon it and smiled. This was my symbol for what I believed in. Peace. Love. A world where your dream is not to kill, but to grow, teach and help people adapt to it. I spent years and years of my youth all the way from ages seven to fifteen wondering what I was to be.

Then on my fifteenth birthday when I received a set of a wrenches, a few nails, a hammer, and some planks I figured out what I wanted to be. I wanted to fix railway lines. If ever a track had a loose screw or needed something done, that's what I wanted to do. My big dream was to work at Marylebone station, and when the Lords and Ladies would rattle past in their huge oak carriages I would wave an oily hand and take off my cap. That was my dream.

It took about a week to reach our destination in France and I couldn't believe where it was.

It was by the Somme river.

For two months nothing happened. It was as they had said: a quiet sector. There were occasional shelling and night patrols, but other than that we left each other alone. In the trenches it was much worse. The conditions were disgusting. Whenever you wanted to move you had to lean on the wall of the trench. At least it was a bit better than the other time we had been there.

It was safer as well as we had dug deeper. There was the ground floor then a platform you would climb up onto for battle.

Our comrades were much worse. They swore and cursed about the mud, and whenever an argument broke out it resulted in a fight. It was as bad as the officers had said. The new recruits, it seemed, had had fifteen weeks of training before arriving here. Whenever I was chosen to go on a night patrol, I would have to stick by them and protect them as best I could. But other than that, they weren't so bad.

I mostly sat hunched in a dugout sheltering from the rain that had started again. But I could tell that something was going to happen soon. Everyone could feel it.

Then, on the twenty-first of March it happened. I heard hundreds of German troops surging across no-man's land. Shells rained down upon us, the earth that was thrown up burying many of us alive. A direct hit on the entrance of the dugout I was in made me fly backwards. I kicked and whacked the stock of my rifle against the fallen wood and mud until a gap appeared. I scrambled out and saw chaos: the whole trench was falling in. Officers were trying to rally their men to stand and fire.

There was no success and further shelling caused us to abandon the trench. The soldiers who stayed were downed and just about then the first enemy soldiers entered our front line almost unopposed.

'Evacuate,' Lieutenant Colonel Frenner bellowed, wrenching his revolver out of his pocket.

I grabbed a trench raiding club, swinging it about wildly. But I quickly gave up defending and joined my comrades as we rushed to our support trench in haste. A machine gun opened fire on a group of us mowing most of us down.

We finally reached the support trench, the supporting battalion there giving us a blank stare.

Lieutenant Colonel Frenner and the officers reorganised their plans as we set up barricades along the communication trench.

We set up machine guns on top of them and waited for the enemy to appear. I crouched down and looked through a gap in the barbed wire barricades we had set up.

'They're coming now,' Major Bennet announced. And so they were. Many of the soldiers started panicking and ran. 'Stand your ground, lads,' Lieutenant Colonel Frenner shouted, drawing a revolver. This was the first time I had seen the officers in combat. 'Fire!' they shouted.

I fired every shot I had on me but still they kept coming. Then I heard explosions.

'Please let it be ours,' I prayed.

It wasn't. It was theirs. Only it came from small heavy guns that had been positioned on their side of the communication trench. All of a sudden, my vision blurred and I blacked out.

'Get up,' a voice whispered. 'Alfie, get up.'

I opened my eyes. 'What?' I said. 'It's pitch black. And where are we.'

'Dugout,' another voice replied. 'Come on. We've got to escape.' I looked around and saw the walls of a dugout. 'Where in the line are we.'

'Reserve trench.' I recognised this voice as Darren's.

'Stop your chatting,' a voice snarled. This was Sergeant First Class Rought. 'We gotta get outta here.'

'Don't you worry, Sarge,' I told him. 'We'll be escaping in a jiffy. Just as soon as I find some ammunition and my rifle.'

'Here, Alf,' Lenny passed me a dozen clips of ammunition and a rifle.

'K,' Sergeant First Class Rought hissed. 'Let's go.'

We snuck out of the dugout and I saw more of our men waiting outside.

'OK,' Lieutenant Colonel Frenner ordered. 'Here's what you're gonna do.'

'Us?' one of the soldiers said loudly.

'Yes you,' Lieutenant Colonel Frenner hissed back.

'Why not you officers?' the soldier answered back.

'Shut up and listen. You're going to be led by Lieutenant Netford. Just do a full out attack on the support trench. And don't stop there. Stop when every single blimmin' man in

113

this battalion is either dead or wounded. Do I make myself clear?'

'Yes, sir,' we all stammered.

'Not one step back,' Lieutenant Colonel Frenner ordered.

We nodded.

'Now go, go, go!'

We set off, under the cover of night, creeping through the trenches until we were in the support trench. I saw German cigarettes lit and heard their mutter. I spotted Lieutenant Netford creeping forward with his revolver until he was seen by a German.

All of a sudden, the Germans opened fire. We covered Lieutenant Netford back to us until we realised he never intended on staying for more than a few seconds. 'Attack,' he panted when he reached us. 'Attack.'

We charged forward with ferocity only to be downed by machine guns. I fired my rifle countless times until the Germans, who had been surprised by our counterattack, fled into our fire trench.

'Bayonet charge,' Lieutenant Netford yelled. 'For king and country!'

We charged towards the Germans shouting 'For king and country' until we had driven them back into their trenches. By the time that day was over, we had lost one third of our battalion.

'Dig,' barked the officers. 'Dig, dig, dig.' In May, we had reclaimed our trenches, but were running low on soldiers, ammunition and food. Only one hundred and fifty remained in our battalion and the rest of us, even the officers would rather doze in the sun or clean our rifles than fix and dig trenches, clean dugouts, and be on sentry duty.

For the past few weeks, we had been spending every hour re-digging our trenches until everything was fine. I had hollowed out a section in a trench where I often slept and it held up with a column of sandbags on each side.

June came and one day, I heard some glorious news. We had a three day leave to relax and have a nice time before an all-out offensive. It wasn't long enough to go home but it was long enough to have a nice long time in a cafe or a 'barre' which is what the French call a 'bar'.

The day they let us leave the trenches everyone headed to the barre and ordered large tankards of beer. We'd down pint after pint, tankard after tankard, laughing and nattering, helmets off, rifles laid down.

We had been allowed a small shabby hotel to stay in whilst we were on leave. The bed sheets were shabby and creased with dust but that didn't matter to us. And the water for their baths was lukewarm but to us it felt steaming hot.

After only one night in a dusty bed with a comfortable pillow, I felt refreshed and ready for the next day. I joined the others to stroll around the town of Amien happy as larks.

For once I was happy. But for only three days.

Those three days were like water trickling through my fingers. I couldn't keep hold of that time. Before I knew it I was back in my uniform, helmet on, rifle presented, with Sergeant First Class Rought inspecting us. He announced that we were lucky to have even received even one day of leave and that we were going to be doing drills and inspections for the rest of the war until he was satisfied that we had been improved by him.

'Attention!' Major Bennet strolled down the ranks of men looking at us. 'Are you aware that Captain Miltain was wounded?' he asked us all.

'Yes, sir,' we replied together.

'Well, I would like to introduce your new captain who shall lead you into battle,' Major Bennet announced. 'Captain Ray. Fresh from Belgium. A battle-hardy officer whom you should all respect.'

Captain Ray marched towards us looking down his nose at us. Bands played as we all saluted him. He smiled, his tongue poking out of his mouth and his beady eyes swiveling around as if he were looking for something.

As soon as Captain Ray took command, he started yelling at us for no apparent reason, sending men into no man's land because they needed to learn some discipline (and because he didn't want to himself). Later, when I learnt how brave and good a leader he could be I forgot all about how he had treated us in the first months of his rule.

The Hundred Day Offensive

'Up your ladders lads,' Captain Ray called. 'C'mon! Up your ladders!'

I stood up one rung on a ladder waiting for the whistle. It was a boiling summer's day in August and we were poised to go over the top. I looked up at the blazing sun and prayed for victory. The whistle blew and we climbed out of our trenches.

'Go, go, go,' Captain Ray shouted. Instead of mud, hot soil crunched under our feet as we neared the enemy.

For about fifteen yards no one got harmed and that was when I found out why: they hadn't known we were coming. Only their sentries spotted us late on.

Shells started hailing down on us and, not a moment too soon, I jumped into a shell hole just as a whizzbang passed me with a whistle.

I crawled towards the top and saw that we were all sheltering in shell holes. All except Captain Ray who waved his revolver as if he were a cowboy and charged forward.

He gave us the courage that no other officer could. He made us laugh as if he were a mad man. And he had still not been hit! As the fire intensified, he took shelter in shell holes popping back out and then in until his helmet was shot off into the open.

He turned to look at us and yelled: 'Well don't just stand there. Move! Move yer flamin' arses.'

Even though we were in the middle of a battle I smiled. We really did have a humorous captain, even in the midst of battle.

The little battalion ploughed through the battlefield until we arrived in their trenches. We had had quite a few casualties but it was over in five minutes.

We didn't stop there though; Captain Ray waved his revolver and bellowed at us to pursue them down their trenches. I charged forward with my bayonet fixed but the stragglers had already surrendered. A machine gun had been set up in a reserve trench by the Germans and was rattling away at us. I threw a grenade at the machine gun and waited for it to explode. Killing the machine gunner and his assistant I charged forward smacking an enemy with my rifle stock.

The Fritz were in full retreat when I noticed an officer dash into a dugout. A flame-trooper blazed his flamethrower burning some of our comrades alive. I charged into the dugout with the officer and noticed there were three stormtroopers loading a small machine gun called an MP18.

I backed out of the dugout but didn't go any further.

A stormtrooper threw a grenade at the entrance to the dugout but I kicked it back wildly just before it exploded. After hearing the explosion, I fired into the dugout five times hoping I'd hit someone. The officer had taken out his revolver as he dragged himself to the shelter of a crate of ammunition.

I figured that I would win a duel if I could get to him, so I fired at him non-stop until I reached him, then unloaded into his chest.

For the next few hours, we charged through the meadows until we reached their artillery.

I ducked down and hid in a shell hole, seeking cover from German fire. A soldier with a Vickers machine gun was punching holes into Germans' chests.

For a few moments I stayed there until I met a private who was sobbing on the floor a shrapnel wound from a grenade in his knee. I dragged him back where I took off my belt and tied it on top of his wound to keep pressure on it.

'It's alright, Private,' I muttered. 'It's terrible what those bastards have done to you.'

He continued sobbing as I motioned for a combat medic to come over and take care of him.

I threw several of my last grenades at a heavy gun, causing it to explode and send metal flying everywhere, catching a dozen Germans.

Panting, I left the trenches to retrieve who I could amongst the fallen before they were hit by shells. For the next two days we continued ploughing forward and we didn't lose a single pace of land.

This was the start of a campaign where next to our allies France and America we continued marching forward, our casualties mounting, but still gaining territory and winning every single battle.

But one of the few days where we really shone was someday in September. We were marching across a battlefield when German biplanes appeared and started strafing us. They zoomed over our heads firing machine guns at us.

'Attack,' Captain Ray yelled as we got up.

I knew the Germans had dug in deep in the trench that we were heading towards but I didn't dare disobey his orders, so I simply fixed my bayonet and joined his charge.

That day we conquered an entire trench and the town that lay beside it. Although there was fierce German resistance with machine guns and rifle fire.

Our battalion was reduced to sixty soldiers.

'Get ready lads,' Captain Ray shouted. 'Big push today. Lucky it's in the fog. Fritz won't have much fun picking us off today, huh? We'll practically be invisible.'

And he was right. We snuck across no man's land like ninjas without a single shot being fired. But when we got about five meters away from their trenches Captain Ray made us dive into shell holes.

For thirty seconds we waited there in case the Germans had spotted us. When we knew they hadn't I saw Captain Ray mouth the words: 'throw grenades.'

I grabbed a grenade and took out the pin. In unison we chucked them into the trenches. For a moment nothing happened until dozens of explosions detonated and Germans staggered out of their trenches cursing.

'Fire!' Captain Ray cried and we did as he said.

We fired at the sentries and enemy soldiers who were peering through the fog. 'Enter the trenches,' Captain Ray commanded. I threw another grenade and waited until it went off.

Quickly, I ran to the parapet and threw myself level with the sandbags.

'Get up, Lance Corporal,' Sergeant First Class Rought shouted, but it was too late.

An enemy soldier plunged his bayonet down and I only just managed to get out of the way. Managing to pin his arm down I heard a crack and saw a bullet wound in his head. He collapsed, killed instantly.

Sergeant First Class Rought hopped into the trench.

Pointing my rifle, I hopped in after him. Due to the fog I couldn't see anyone unless they were close to me as we hunted the Germans in the trenches.

I was searching a dugout when it happened. I saw a line of string running along the entrance and was surprised that I hadn't trodden on it. I heard Captain Ray come in and ask me if I had found anything before I heard the sound of moving feet and a crumbling sound.

Then, all at once an explosion took place that shattered the dugout walls and ceiling. Debris and plaster splattered onto me, along with splintering tiles.

'Sir,' I gasped, trying not to inhale too much dust. 'C'mon. We need to get out of here.'

Then I saw him. Captain Ray had been buried in dust, timber, and tiles. Grabbing his left leg and yanking it, I pulled him out of the dugout. He didn't revive and we had to leave him in the mist.

The trenches were a battle scene. The Germans had counter-attacked and we, in turn, were pushing forward until they retreated.

That day had left the battalion distressed. For some reason and although I had protested and said what I had done was only normal they awarded me the Victoria Cross for saving Captain Ray and Captain Miltain and all the others.

So now I had two Victoria Crosses that I didn't think I needed, and I was made to wear them on my uniform along with the Albert Medal, the Distinguished Conduct Medal, and the Victory Medal (everyone in the battalion had been awarded that as we had been victorious). We had been pulled out of the line to rest, but soon we were put back in again and I was sure I knew why. A small town had been recaptured by the Germans and we had to be out back into the line of trenches near that town. A machine-gunning post brilliantly covered for snipers and rifle men, making it a real bastion.

We waited for a few weeks to attack but then we had some news.

It was October now and Germany had sent a request to America's President Woodrow Wilson seeking an armistice. That was as much as we knew but we were sure that Germany would do what he requested for peace.

We celebrated by passing tiny footballs between each other and drinking deep into the night in our dugouts.

Whenever tanks or aircraft rumbled by we would wave our hands energetically, waving white handkerchiefs and grinning. Of course this wasn't very often but it gave us courage.

We were also greeted by the return of Captain Miltain, who settled straight back into his dugout, smoking and thinking.

Everything was becoming less and less common, sniper fire, machine gun fire, rifle fire, artillery fire. Night raids were stopping altogether but we were still fighting. And I knew we were going to have to go over the top again.

But the war was ending.

I could tell.

I hadn't written to Mother for about a month so huddling beside a small fire I wrote her a cheerful letter saying that the war was soon going to be over.

Dearest Mother,

I hope you are well, as I am. The war is certain to be over soon. I reckon it shall be before Christmas. Everything is lessening, the gunfire, the night patrols, even the moods are changing, more of us are chatting to each other than sleeping. The mood is definitely less grim.

For some reason I have been awarded the Victoria Cross - I don't know why. All I did was drag someone out of a dugout and drag another person into our trenches. It doesn't sound like much if you think about it.

But then the officers said that this was also because I had saved "many" other soldiers, but that was about one or two years ago. I can't remember. It's been so long.

If we are attacked by Fritz it'll be a one man job. There are now only about sixty of us so they may as well forget it. Don't you worry though. I'm jolly well fine and I shall get through this war alive.

May you ask Fred how he is? I do miss his grunting in the trenches when he dozed. Is he used to a wooden leg?

I send you my best from France, Alfie

I looked at it, nodded, and pressed it to my heart. Then I took out of my chest pocket the photograph of me, Fred, Harley, Father and Mother. And Mango in the background.

I closed my eyes and drifted off to sleep in a dugout.

The Eleventh Hour of the Eleventh Day of the Eleventh Month

'Peace!' The voice rang out that morning. 'Fritz signed an armistice. At eleven on the dot the war's over, lads.'

'Well, I'm afraid it's a little late for that, lads,' Major Bennet told us. 'We got our orders that we're attacking that machine gunning post this morning. Then if we take it we're gonna try to take the town next to it.'

'But, sir,' I implored.

'What?' Major Bennet snapped.

'If the war is gonna be over at eleven what's the point of dying when it's nearly over.'

'Shut up!' Major Bennet snarled. 'You got your orders and you're gonna do them. Led by Lieutenant Netford and Sergeant First Class Rought. And you're going over the top at .. let's see,' he checked his watch… 'In thirty minutes.. so get ready. Our machine guns are already keeping them busy. Hurry up!' And he left the men to stare at each other in shock.

'I thought I was gonna get to see my sister again,' one of the soldiers said.

'I thought I was gonna get to see my mother again,' one of the other soldiers said.

'I thought I was gonna get to see the end of the war.'

Those thirty minutes went far too quickly for my liking and I soon found myself with my rifle in my hands, loaded and ready.

Then Lieutenant Netford got a whistle in his mouth and blew it, signaling us to scramble out of the trench towards the machine gunning post.

The firing was rapid, unending fire, mowing down one third of our battalion. I fired quickly and never sought cover because I knew that if I did when I reemerged I would be a bigger target.

Once I had reached a line of wire fifty yards from the Germans I pulled out a grenade to throw. Fumbling with the pin I threw it at the enemy and heard the explosion.

Somehow, enough of our battalion had survived the machine guns to overrun the Germans and push them into the town.

But now the battalion was more like a section of twenty men, with no one ranked above sergeant. (Sergeant First Class Rought had been hit by machine gunfire as had Lieutenant Netford.)

The man who took control was Sergeant Bradshort. He rallied us up and led us into the deserted town where we searched for Germans.

Unfortunately, we lost two soldiers hit by sniper fire and five by a stray soldier we had picked up. We took cover behind a wall in case the Germans were there, then headed through the archway.

I kicked open the door of a house and aimed my rifle. We filed in, finding a family of three - a small boy of six, and his parents.

The child wanted to follow us as we searched the house and alerted us when we heard gunshots.

'Excuse me, mister soldiers?' he said. 'There are gunshots. Hurry.'

We jumped out of the house and looked down the street.

Just then tears of blood welled up on one soldier's chest and he fell to the ground.

'Go, go, go,' Sergeant Bradshort ordered.

We rushed down the street and met the Germans around the corner. I fired a shot at a kneeling German but hit a shattered lantern instead.

I fired again and again at them, ducking, then lying down. It was an intense fight, until we threw grenades and they disappeared down an alleyway.

We pursued them into a deserted house where they shot out of the windows. I ducked down behind a car with smoke coming from it. Praying they didn't have expert aim I revealed my face and fired my rifle at a German. It hit and I ducked down to reload again. This time I threw a grenade but it fell short.

We pursued the garrison into a field with small trenches where they took cover. We didn't halt as it would only slow us down.

Instead, Sergeant Bradshort ordered us to charge and take the trench. But due to their machine guns we took cover in the houses firing at exposed heads.

I ran forward taking cover beside a small bush and covered a soldier who had a Vickers machine gun.

I ran forward, and as Sergeant Bradshort ran forward with his men the Germans evacuated the trench.

Taking cover in the shallow trench I loaded a new clip into my magazine as a Vickers machine gunner rattled at German heads poking out from another trench they had retreated to.

There wasn't much cover, so you had to lie on your front to make yourself less visible.

As a lump of dirt was blown into the air by a bullet I stood up and fired, noticing Lenny crawling forward on his stomach. Sergeant Bradshort ordered us to attack once more and when we did, the Germans abandoned that trench too.

And so it went on, until we came to the end of the field and they entered a barn, supposedly to reload and take cover.

They suddenly charged at us, catching us by surprise, so we abandoned the trench before turning around and taking it back with close combat fighting. Again, the remains of the German unit escaped to the barn.

'C'mon,' Sergeant Bradshort yelled. 'May as well fight to the last man.'

We followed him towards the barn where I spotted riflemen and snipers firing.

The huge wooden doors were locked so with the help of grenades and bayonets we made holes in the doors.

I lobbed a grenade into the barn and saw the explosion light up the room.

'Go, go, go,' I saw a Corporal whispering urgently to a Vickers machine gunner who was setting it up in one of the holes in the doors.

He fired into the room before he was shot in the head and a grenade destroyed his gun, making the gap big enough for us to enter.

I jumped in and ducked down behind a huge bale of hay. More of us entered and I saw Darren enter last, covered by everyone else.

A ladder led to the second floor where snipers were concealed and picking us off.

Crouched down, I waddled forward about five yards before finding myself facing a German.

Before he could point his rifle at me I smacked it out of his hands with my rifle stock and put a finger to my mouth.

Somehow, I prodded him to Sergeant Bradshort who assigned a private to guard him whilst I took his rifle.

Eventually, we disposed of them and found ourselves lying on the grass, listening. And then we heard it. The sound we hadn't heard for four whole years.

Bells rang out over the entire world and we all felt that same sense of happiness and relief we felt whenever we returned to the reserved trench.

I was lying next to Lenny and Darren and I said, 'We did it guys. We did it. The Pengies lived through the Great War to see another generation.'

'Yeah,' Darren said. 'Tell me about it. This is a tale to tell our grandchildren.'

'Yeah,' Lenny said. 'Specially for you, Alf.'

'What?' I asked.

'Y'know. Winning the DCM, Albert Medal and the Victoria Cross. Saving about two million people. And being promoted to Lance Corporal after less than a year at the front line.'

'Oh shut up,' I told him, grinning.

'Anyway,' Darren changed the subject. 'Twenty-one years old we are. And I haven't had a girl yet. Not one sweetheart.'

'Oh, I've got plenty of options,' I smirked. 'I've got my lovely Mara, haven't I.'

'And I've got myself,' Lenny laughed. 'I'm not marrying. I'm being a godfather, right?'

'Hmm,' I mused. 'I'm not so sure about that. I reckon it might be Darren. I want my kids to have a mature role model.'

'Oh you shut up,' Lenny said.

'This world is going to be so different,' Darren sighed.

'So are we,' Lenny smirked. 'After we've had a bath.'

We all cackled there on that meadow until we were ordered to get the wounded and return to our trenches.

The trenches were full of celebration where we sang until our throats were saw. But we couldn't relax now.

The next morning the officers told us we were going into the town to help the refugees move back into their homes and fix things up a bit.

I didn't mind that in the slightest as we were the ones who had destroyed their homes. But when I realized for the first time how big a mess and destruction the town was in I knew that I would have to work twice as hard.

We spent all day helping French refugees back into their homes and securing places that had been dangerous before. I pushed a wheelbarrow back into a house full of possessions and laid them on the table where a baby was being fed. Lenny and I lifted up a door and fitted it back onto a frame.

'Tiring work this,' Lenny panted, wiping his brow.

I didn't mind. I just kept working. These people needed help. I climbed up a ladder to help soldiers fix tiles back onto the roof of a church. It took forever; the rest of the day in fact.

A few weeks later we had done what we could. We had long since left the trenches and were staying in tents in a field with a makeshift stable for the officers' horses and single tents for the officers.

One day nearing Christmas we were told happy news. Captain Miltain had trotted up to us on his horse whilst we stood stiff, saluting.

'At ease,' he said.

Relaxing, we listened to his news.

'We'll take the train from here to the Calais docks. Then the next day we'll board the ferry and let it take us to Blighty. In two days you'll be in Blighty on the train back to London.'

Everyone in our small battalion grinned at each other and started cheering. This time tomorrow we'd be at the docks waiting for the ferry. I couldn't wait.

Before we left I still had to clean out the stables, and groom and feed the horses. Of course, I did Big Red first. He was still my favorite horse and he seemed to like me.

I made sure he had plenty of oats and water then replaced his hay with some fresh hay then moved on to the next horse; a midnight black stallion, that had the strength of a gorilla. That evening we had a toast to all the fallen in this war.

I had held my beer bottle as high up as anyone before I took a deep swig.

Silently I toasted Harley and Walter (the German soldier who had tried to stab me) as I knew they were the bravest people I would ever set eyes upon.

Home

'Hoot, hoot!' The train steamed.

'Get on,' Lieutenant Colonel Frenner ordered. 'Hurry up.'

Boarding the train, I felt a new sense of happiness. I entered a carriage and sat down by the window, staring in the direction of the English Channel, the direction of home.

'All right there, Alf?' Lenny asked, sitting down next to me.

'Yeah,' I said in a dreamy voice. 'Yeah. I'm fine.'

'You'd better be. Blighty's only a few hours away till you can see it'.

And he was right. After about five hours when the train hissed and the doors clacked open I saw the mist of the English Channel. And if you looked close enough, England.

We stayed the night in a small field, officers in the shacks around it, us just lying under the stars, left to the mercy of December's weather. We lit a huge fire and with the help of cushioning from our rucksack we managed to fall into a cold, shallow sleep.

The next morning we arrived at the dock and waited for the ferry. It was a misty day with a cool breeze making us shiver. To pass the time I lit a cigarette and smoked until I saw the hull of the ferry dock.

We boarded and to everyone's surprise Captain Miltain asked Lieutenant Colonel Frenner whether or not we could throw our weapons into the water as a sign of peace.

He said we couldn't do that but we could throw a grenade each into the water.

We took out our grenades and chucked them all into the water. A rally of machine gun fire finished the show off and we returned to our seats.

I started to feel restless after a while and went onto the deck to look at Blighty. The mist had cleared a little and I could see the faint outline of the cliffs of Dover.

'See that Lenny?' I said excitedly. 'Dover. You can see Dover.'

He looked and spotted it too. 'Then we can't be far from the coast.'

'I should get my parading cap on,' I said, joking.

'I never knew we had them.'

'Seriously?'

'Wait, I might have it in my rucksack.'

'Good. I can see the harbour.'

I had barely muttered the words when a sailor on the ship yelled, 'Land ahoy!'

We all cheered at that and bunched up on the deck only to see crowds of people awaiting us carrying roses and all sorts of flowers, cakes and armfuls of delicious-looking food. All of them were cheering. When we had docked and exited the ship a stampede of flamboyant colours met my eyes. We marched all the way to the train station, where hundreds more people were waiting.

I accepted a large bottle of wine that an excited but nervous boy pushed into my hand. He also gave me a letter, the most thoughtful letter I have ever read. It went like this.

Dear brave soldier,

My name is Elliot. I am eight years old. I think that you are very brave for going to fight for your country and I admire you. Please. Have this bottle of wine and fifty pence as a sign of our gratitude. And please can you tell me what your name is?

I looked at him astonished.

'Alfie,' I told him. 'My name is Alfie Tuck.'

Elliot beamed at me and ran off to his parents.

At the train station I received many more presents, most of them given by children. They would walk up to us with beer or wine or whisky or a cake and simply give them to us. One boy of eleven walked up to me and asked if he could hold my rifle.

I said he could but couldn't fire any shots. In fact, I let him rifle through my kit as we waited for the train, so several minutes later, he was wearing my helmet, and holding the rifle the way I showed him we did for kit inspection. His parents took a photograph of us together.

Eventually, the train steamed in and the doors clacked open. The boy returned my kit and we boarded the train.

'Can you believe that?' Lenny asked as we settled down in a carriage.

'No,' Darren said.

'All those people just for me,' Lenny exclaimed.

'Not just you,' Darren told him.

'Can you believe how many drinks I've got?' Lenny said. 'I think it's about one beer, one big bottle of wine and a Guinness.'

'Same here,' I said. 'One child tried on my helmet and held my rifle. He went loony.'

'Everyone was too busy buying me drinks,' Lenny sighed.

'Yeah right,' Darren snorted.

'Yup,' Lenny agreed. 'Yeah.'

The train hissed to a stop and I jerked awake.

'Get up, you two,' Darren pinched Lenny and me.

'Wassup?' Lenny grunted.

'We're back in Penge. We're home.'

In an instant Lenny's eyes were open and he sat up straight. I staggered out of the carriage and off the train. I heard a yell that I didn't recognise at first.

'Alfie. Alfie.'

I turned to the sound of my name and there they were. Mother, Fred and Mara. I ran up to them and hugged them. Fred clapped me on the soldier and I looked at his legs. There were wooden legs on which he was standing on.

'Alfie!' he grinned.

'Frederick,' I grinned back.

I turned to Mother who was beaming, her eyes filled to the brim with tears of happiness.

'Hello, Mother,' I said joyfully.

'Alfie,' she breathed as if it were a dream.

'It's all right,' I reassured her and we hugged.

Lastly, I hugged Mara who whispered in my ear, 'Long time, no see.'

I grinned.

'Good to see you soldier.'

18 Years later: 1936

France. How long has it been? Nineteen years. I can't believe it. I look down at my two children, Elliot (named after the boy in the streets who had shown such kindness to me) and Alice. They are twins except that Elliot is older by one minute. They are the things I treasure most in the entire world.

I had wanted to name Elliot Harley after Harley but Mara had declined it and said that Elliot was a much cuter name and it was good to remember people who did small things.

The blisters on my heels ache as we trek up the hill. Alice is holding a map and directing us. Elliot is firing questions at me. At last we arrive at the place I have wanted to go to for years:

Guillemont Road Cemetery.

We push past the gate and enter the graveyard. Elliot and Alice hunt the grave we are looking for, looking at every single one and asking me if I know any of them. Most of them I don't.

I take out the photograph and look at Harley, his short hair and enthusiastic grin. I tuck it back into my pocket.

'I see it!' Elliot and Alice yell in unison.

I look up and run over to them, where they are kneeling at a gravestone. I scan the worn-out inscription on it and give a start.

Private H. M. Tuck
Royal West Kent Regiment
3rd September 1916
DCM

Beneath that is a cross with a Distinguished Conduct Medal shaped on it.

'Is that him? Is that him?' Elliot jabbers.

'Yes, Elliot,' I reply quietly. 'That is him.'

'What did he look like?' Alice asks thoughtfully.

'A bit like me,' I answer somberly. 'A bit like you too Elliot. And you Alice. Got that look on your face.'

'You remember him, Mara?' I call over to her.

'Yes,' she replies, walking up to us. 'Quite a boy, wasn't he?'

'Yeah,' Elliot says. 'You told me he saved your life, Dad. Did he?'

'Yes. He did. I was being stupid in the face of death and he paid the price for it.'

'What did you do?' Alice asks, fascinated.

'Later,' I say. 'I tell you what. I'll buy you a bag of sweets to share and we can talk all about that later. Sound good?'

'Good,' they grin at the prospect of having sweets. Anything that has sugar is OK with them.

I take out a small shovel and dig a hole in the ground. Then I take out the Victoria Cross I was 'awarded' by the refugee in Belgium and lay it down to rest there. Then I take out a poppy wreath and lay it on the grave.

'See you, Harley,' I whisper, wiping tears from my eyes.

Mara leads the children away whilst I have my last words with Harley telling him all about the world he has helped create.

At last, I follow Mara and leave Harley alone.

'So…' Elliot prompts as soon as we sit down, chewing on a flake.

'So what?' I ask, sighing, opening a bottle of beer.

'You were going to tell us how he saved you,' Alice reminds me.

'Ah yes,' I recall. So I tell them the whole story. How I jumped the wire and caught my foot in it.

How Harley had come to my aid and was shot by the machine gunner.

When I had finish, Elliot starts with his rapid five-question-a-minute routine. When my story is over Elliot and Alice turn to Mara who seems pleased they aren't eating chocolate and sweets because they are listening so carefully. (Mara never has been one for sweets. I have tried to see eye to eye with her on this but can't even imagine not having mint humbugs and flakes.)

As she tells them all about the horrible things she witnessed at the hospital I see her in a whole different light.

I knew that she had seen dreadful things and saved many lives, but I hadn't pictured her, standing there with medicine in her hand or administering dressing to a soldier's wounds.

I just couldn't until then. Maybe I was too absorbed in the horrors echoing in my head.

When we're done we return to the place we are staying at, before returning to England. I work as a railway engineer, just as I had dreamed.

But it is not the same world as it had been before the Great War. In fact, it is far from the same. It is a different world due to the war. But I lived through it. And I don't want to have to live through anything like that again.

About the author

Jackson Wild was born in Johannesburg, South Africa. At the age of five, he and his family moved to Penge, South East London. There Jackson goes to Alexandra Junior School and is preparing for secondary school. He enjoys researching the war, but also likes having sleepovers with his best friends, Arthur, Ella and Stanley Driver.

Lightning Source UK Ltd.
Milton Keynes UK
UKHW010847030522
402369UK00006B/82